W9-BRJ-818

"Help!" I yelled. "Help! Mr. Maples! Mr. Jones! Help!"

They wouldn't hear me, I knew, but I had to try. It was easier than beating the door down.

I tried to stare through the inky blackness, but I couldn't. I'd never seen darkness so thick. It made my stomach churn. So did the thought of spiders running around in here . . . spiders that I couldn't see.

If I could find the door, I would find the light switch. But in the instant darkness, my sense of direction was all out of whack. I had no idea where the door was.

I shuddered and pain ripped up my arm. Something was broken. It had to be. I'd heard a crack when I hit the box, and the bursts of pain every time my arm moved were terrible.

The East Edge Mysteries
  • The Secret of the Burning House
  • Discovery at Denny's Deli

THE SECRET OF THE
BURNING HOUSE

GAYLE ROPER

Chariot Books™
David C. Cook Publishing Co.

Published by Chariot Books,
an imprint of David C. Cook Publishing Co.
David C. Cook Publishing Co., Elgin, Illinois 60120
David C. Cook Publishing Co., Weston, Ontario
Nova Distribution, Ltd., Newton Abbot, England

THE SECRET OF THE BURNING HOUSE
© 1992 by Gayle G. Roper

All rights reserved. Except for brief excerpts for review purposes, no
part of the book may be reproduced or used in any form without
written permission from the publisher.

Cover illustration by Cindy Webber
Cover design by Helen Lannis
First printing, 1992
Printed in the United States of America
96 95 94 93 92 5 4 3 2 1

Library of Congress Cataloging-in-Publication Data
Roper, Gayle G.
The secret of the burning house/Gayle Roper.
p. cm.—(An East Edge mystery)
Summary: Unhappy about being forced to move to East Edge,
twelve-year-old Dee finds that God is everywhere when an arsonist
strikes the house of her new friend Cammi.
ISBN 1-55513-695-8
[1. Moving, Household—Fiction. 2. Arson—Fiction. 3. Christian
life—Fiction. 4. Mystery and detective stories.]
I. Title. II. Series: Roper, Gayle G.   East edge mystery.
PZ7.R6788Se   1992
[Fic]—dc20
                                            92-5091
                                            CIP
                                            AC

for those special young ladies
Carolyn, Laurel, and Kelly

1

EAST EDGE MYSTERIES

What an ugly house, I thought. *I hate it.*

"What a lovely house!" said Mom. "Oh, Dee, don't you just love it?" She gave my shoulders a squeeze.

We Dennings stood in the driveway of our new home. It was ten at night, and we had just driven eleven hours. We were all feeling hot and achy. I was also feeling cranky.

Stupid white house. Dumb black shutters. I frowned.

"I think the black shutters make the white shingles look so clean," said Mom. "We're so fortunate!"

I looked at Mom to see if she were joking. She had to be joking. Mom always looked at the bright side of things, but this was ridiculous. Fortunate? We were in East Edge, Pennsylvania, hundreds of miles from where I wanted to be. We were about to move into a white house with black shutters and a bright red door, for Pete's sake.

"Don't you love that red door?" asked Mom. "It's so bright and cheery and inviting!"

"Inviting? It's embarrassing," I muttered. But Mom didn't hear. She and Dad were going up the steps to the awful red door. Phil and Mike, my eight-year-old twin brothers, trailed behind.

I dragged myself up the walk, thinking about the nice brick ranch we had left behind in Indiana, of Allison and Mandy whom I'd probably never see again and of the big elms with the hammock where I liked to lie and stare at the clouds and wonder about things.

"Deanna, honey," Dad had said last night, "I know you don't want to move. I know you don't like change, and eleven is a particularly hard age for such big changes. But God has called me to pastor a new church, and we have to go. You must remember that circumstances change and seem bad, but God is always with us—and He never changes. Besides, I know you'll like East Edge once we get there."

I had stared at Dad and not said anything, but inside I was screaming. *How come God never asked me about this move? Is it fair that I have to move because you want to?*

"It'll be all right, Sunshine," Dad had said, calling me by my pet name. When I was little, he used to sing "You Are My Sunshine" to me because, he would say, "You're such a happy child, always shining and sunny."

I didn't feel sunny now. Dark storm clouds thundered in my heart and mind, and I wanted to cry. I stepped into the hall of the new house, taking care not to look at the red door. It was hotter inside than out . . . and out was very hot on this July Friday night.

"Turn on the air conditioning," I said. "It's a furnace in here."

Dad fiddled with a dial, and with a quiet roar the central air conditioning came to life. Almost immediately, with a louder roar, it died.

"Uh oh," said Dad. He headed for the cellar door and disappeared down the steps.

Phil and Mike followed him, offering useless suggestions.

"Deanna, your room's upstairs," said Mom. "Let's go look at it. We can plan where to put your furniture, so we'll know what to tell the moving men when they get here tomorrow."

"My room's in Indiana," I said, but Mom was already halfway upstairs. After a minute, I sighed and followed her. My room was to the left of the stairs, across the hall from the bathroom. The walls were a creamy yellow with teddy bears stenciled around the ceiling. "Mom! Teddy bears?"

"This was the baby's room for the last family who lived here. Give us time to settle, and we'll redo things to make it your room."

"Mine's in Indiana." I felt very stubborn and angry.

Mom walked over and put her arm around me, but instead of leaning in for comfort, I pulled away. I didn't want to feel better. I wanted to go home.

"Come on, honey," said Mom. "Let's carry in the sleeping bags and the things we need for tonight. We can camp out in the living room. It's got a nice, soft carpet."

"What color?" I asked.

"Blue."

"I don't like blue. I'll sleep up here."

Mom smiled, crinkling the corners of her eyes, and nodded. "If you'd like."

I refused to smile back.

"Dee, it's not like you to be moody. Try to look for good things in the move."

"Like what?"

"Like an exciting new job for Dad. Like new opportunities for you."

I frowned. "I don't want new opportunities. I want to live in Indiana. I want to go home!"

"Honey," said Mom softly, "you are home." She smiled encouragingly and went downstairs. I looked around my empty room. It looked as forlorn as I felt. I ran my hand despairingly through my hair, lifting my bangs off my forehead and blowing upward to cool my wet forehead.

With much bumping and thumping and "I'll beat you!", the twins raced upstairs and charged into my room.

"Out!" I cried. "This is my room!"

"Touchy, aren't we?" said Phil.

"Besides, who wants this one?" said Mike. "It's too little."

"It's cozy," I said, suddenly defensive.

"Cute teddy bears," said Phil. "Real cute."

I glared. Sarcasm in an eight year old is not amusing.

"Too little," repeated Mike.

"Cozy!" I yelled at their backs as they went in search of their room. I suddenly realized I was acting like I wanted this room. "Too little," I muttered. "Dumb teddy bears."

When the front doorbell rang, I jumped. The boys rushed down the steps, but I didn't. I didn't care who it was. I didn't want to meet anyone in Pennsylvania.

"Pizza!" yelled the boys. "Hey, Mom, Dad, it's pizza." The scent of the pizza floated up the steps, and I felt my mouth start watering. My stomach suddenly felt empty.

"Dee!" yelled Mike. "It's pizza! Someone sent us a couple of pizzas."

"Who cares?" I yelled back, but I came downstairs anyway.

"Look," said Mike, peering at the box top. "There's a note."

Mom pulled it off and read aloud, "Welcome, Dennings! Hope the timing on this pizza is about right. Sleep tight and we'll see you in the morning. P.S. There are paper plates in the kitchen and sodas in the refrigerator." She smiled as she handed the paper to Dad. "It's signed 'Your Calvary Church family.' "

The boys raced to the kitchen, and by the time

12

I dragged myself to the table, they had the plates, napkins, paper cups, and sodas in place. The twins ate with enjoyment, as did Mom and Dad. To my surprise, I ate three pieces, but I refused to enjoy them.

It wasn't until I lay down on top of my sleeping bag and tried to sleep that I began to cry. I was so hot, so lonely, so uncertain. I buried my face in my pillow so no one would hear me. Not that anyone would care. They all seemed glad to be here. Well, why not? The boys had each other. Mom and Dad had each other. I was the odd one out. I rolled onto my back and looked at the teddy bears marching around my room. Tears trickled out of my eyes and into my ears. Sometime later, as I tried for the fourth time to count the teddy bears, I fell asleep.

I woke to screaming sirens, the brilliance of flames dancing on my walls, and smoke filling the air.

I sat straight up. *I've got to get out of here!*

I stumbled out of my sleeping bag, still half asleep, and stood there weaving. Where was I? I was beginning to panic when Phil and Mike raced into my room.

"Come and see!"

"We've got to get out of here!" I shouted. I reached for their hands. They ducked away from me and ran back to their room.

"Come on!" they yelled. "This is a great place to watch."

Suddenly I was awake enough for the truth to sink in. It wasn't our house that was on fire. I slumped against the door in relief. Then I felt really guilty, because if it wasn't our house, it was someone else's. While I was being happy for us, someone else was being very sad and scared.

"Dee? Are you all right?" It was Mom, who had come upstairs to check on us.

"I thought it was us when I first woke up." I shivered in the heat.

She nodded. "Me, too."

We went into the boys' room, and the four of us tried to watch out their window. It didn't work too well because we kept getting in each other's way.

Two houses down, on the other side of the street, flames were shooting out of the roof of a house that looked just like the ranch we'd left in Indiana. Some firemen rushed into the house through the front door, their hoses going full blast. Two others were on the roof, hacking at the shingles, trying to make holes.

"To release the heat and smoke," said Phil, as though he knew what he was talking about.

The noise was overwhelming. The roar of engines, voices yelling, car and truck doors slamming, and static from the radio of the police car parked beneath our window filled the night. The leaves rustled in the air currents set up by the heat, and soaring over all else was the hungry crackle of the fire. I was hypnotized by the red and gold tongues that tried to eat anything within their reach. We could see the silhouettes of the firemen using their hoses to keep the fire back—the way a lion tamer uses his whip.

Suddenly, with a loud bang and leap of flame, the roof over the garage fell in. Sparks flew up, and everything became bright as day. Quickly it died down, and the remaining fire looked dull by comparison.

"What caused that explosion?" I asked, trying to see through Phil's head.

"I think a car just blew up," he said.

"How do you know that?" I demanded.

He shrugged. "The same way I know everything. I'm smart." He turned and grinned at me to see if I bought his explanation. I figured he was probably right about the car because he really is smart, but I could never let him know. It was hard enough keeping ahead of a younger brother genius without letting him guess how hard it was.

"I watched a show on TV about fires a couple of weeks ago," he said. "Besides, if it was the garage roof that fell in, it makes sense, doesn't it?"

I didn't answer. *Poor Mike,* I thought. *He has to be Phil's twin. I only have to be his sister.*

Five people and a huge dog huddled in the street near the fire chief's car with its flashing lights. When the roof collapsed, the woman brought her hand to her mouth, then turned and buried her face in the man's chest. A skinny boy, almost as tall as the man, watched with slumped shoulders while he held the dog's leash. The dog was hiding behind the kid's legs. A girl about my age and a boy about the twins' size leaned against the adults.

I pointed. "I bet it's their house."

Mom nodded. "What a terrible thing, to stand and watch your house burn."

"Hey!" Phil pointed to a familiar-looking figure down on the curb. "There's Dad. Let's go stand with him!"

"Shorts!" yelled Mom as the guys flew down the hall. They stopped with a whoop and ran back, grabbed their shorts from where they had tossed them when they got ready for bed, and raced away again.

"I'm going to go down, too," I told Mom. When she didn't object, I threw on some clothes and hurried out to join Dad and the boys. It was amazing how much hotter it was outside where nothing blocked the heat of the fire. I looked at the

17

firemen in their heavy coats and hats. How could they stand them? And where had all the spectators come from? It was three in the morning, for Pete's sake.

"Mr. Denning!" We all jumped. Who around here knew Dad?

"Mr. Denning!" A man was pushing through the crowds of people, waving wildly at us. "I'm so glad you're here," the man said. "The Restons need you." He began pumping Dad's hand. "In case you don't remember me, I'm Mike Picardy."

"I remember," Dad said. "And I assume that's the Restons' house?" Dad pointed to the fire.

Mr. Picardy nodded. "Terrible thing. Terrible. Brooke, you wait here with the pastor's kids. I'll be back in a minute."

For the first time I became aware of a girl about my age. We looked at each other. She had on Madras shorts and a T-shirt, and her hair was combed! I was afraid to look at what I was wearing, and I knew my hair had declared independence and was running wild. Naturally curly hair does that, no matter how you cut it.

"Hi," I said. "I'm Dee."

"D? The letter?" She didn't sniff, but she might as well have.

"No, Dee, D-E-E, short for Deanna."

"Oh." She nodded. "Okay. I'm Brooke."

I made myself smile. "Do you live around here?"

"Do I live here?" Brooke seemed startled. "On this street?"

I nodded.

"Good grief, no."

I looked up and down the block. It looked fine to me. Aside from the house that was fast becoming cinders, everything looked neat and cared for. There were all kinds of houses—Cape Cods like ours, ranches, two-story Colonials, and even a Victorian or two. Maybe when the sun shone, I'd see they were all falling apart, but I didn't think so.

"I live in Chartwell Chase," Brooke announced.

I knew I was supposed to be impressed, but I had no idea what Chartwell Chase was. "Oh," I said. "Okay."

Neither of us said anything for a few seconds. We stood awkwardly side by side and watched the firemen. Already the fire was dead, and they were gathering up some of their equipment. I decided I'd try to talk with Brooke again. I didn't think Dad would want me to dislike the first person I met in East Edge.

"Do you go to my Dad's new church?"

Brooke looked at me. "Your father is the new pastor at *my* church," she said. She turned and walked quickly in the direction her father had gone, and I made no move to stop her. She made me feel like an ant she wanted to step on. When she was lost in the shifting crowd, I gathered up nerve and looked at my clothes. It wasn't as bad as I had feared, but somehow I knew it wasn't good enough for Chartwell Chase.

I looked at the Restons' house. The fire was out, but smoke still puffed into the air like steam from a boiling tea kettle. I could see Dad talking to the family with the dog. Mr. Picardy was there, too, and Brooke and the twins.

I was alone on the curb. Well, almost alone. There was a man standing beside me, wringing his hands, and I felt sad that he was so upset. I guessed he must know the Restons well or something. Suddenly the man laughed. The sound startled me, and I looked at him.

I had been wrong about two things. One, he wasn't a man. He was a tall kid with big hands, maybe a senior in high school or something. Two, he wasn't wringing his hands in distress; he was rubbing them together with glee.

"Hey, Tree!" called two guys walking away from all the activity. "Come on! Your ride's leaving! The excitement's over!"

The tall guy named Tree waved to them. The camera hanging around his neck on a leather strap bounced with each arm swing. "Coming," he called.

He smiled in my direction. "Great fire, wasn't it?" He said it happily, like the twins might say, "Great TV show, wasn't it?" He patted his camera and smiled a secret smile. "Yes, sir, the best. I got some great pictures." He winked at me and loped off after his friends.

The guy gave me the creeps.

When I woke up Saturday morning, the first things I saw were the marching teddy bears. I groaned and rolled on my side—and saw Cammi Reston and Beast asleep on my bedroom floor.

Memory tumbled back like water spilling over a dam. After the strange guy who liked fires had left last night, Mom had come out and joined me on the curb. We were standing there talking about going back to bed when Dad arrived with the Restons and the Picardys in tow. Mr. Picardy and Brooke looked perky and alert. All the Restons looked lost and sad. Cammi and her little brother Hal were crying.

"Sandy," Dad said to Mom, "Cammi and Hal and Beast are going to stay with us tonight." He placed his hands on the shoulders of the girl and the younger brother and smiled at the dog. "The rest of the family is going with the Picardys."

Mom nodded, invited everyone in, and managed to find enough soda left from dinner to give us all a drink. When I led Cammi up to my room, Beast followed, and no one minded. Cammi stood in the doorway and looked at the empty room.

"I used to baby-sit for the family who owned this house," she said. "During the day or sometimes in the early evening if my mom was at home." Cammi smiled. "The baby who lived in this room was the cutest little thing."

We lay in the darkness, waiting for sleep, and I tried to imagine what it must be like to have your house burn down. I knew how it felt to leave your house, and it wasn't good. But I got to pack all my things carefully. I knew the movers would come and give them all back to me. Any things I lost during the move were things I chose to throw away.

Cammi didn't have anything anymore. How do you feel when you have nothing? I looked at Cammi and saw she was fast asleep. Apparently tired was how you felt. Worn out. Well, me too. I slept.

Now, in the morning light, I could see that

Cammi was awake and she was quietly crying. Beast lay pressed against her, and she had her arms wrapped around his neck.

"What kind of dog is he?" I asked.

"A Newfoundland," she said, her voice all quavery.

"He's huge! I bet he rules your family."

"No," she said. "Bugs does." And she began to cry again.

I sighed inwardly. I'd met two girls in East Edge so far. One was a snob and the other cried all the time. Not that she didn't have reason to cry, but it was still trying. I'm not good at being nice like Mom is.

"Don't cry," I said. "It'll be all right. No one was hurt or anything."

"I know." She sniffed. "And I'm glad. But Bugs is missing. And my doll collection! I had over forty dolls."

Forty dolls? Who would want forty dolls? Was there room in her bedroom for her or just her dolls? Maybe she slept on the floor because the dolls had the bed.

"And all my clothes!" she continued. "What do I wear? And Doug's computer and his glasses and his and our bikes and Mom's uniforms and Dad's school papers. But mostly I'm worried about Bugs."

"Who's Bugs? Another dog?"

Cammi shook her head. "He's my cat. He's big and gray and fluffy, and he's missing!"

"Don't cry, Cammi," said a little scared voice. "He's okay. Daddy said so. He's just hiding in the woods behind the house because he's afraid."

Cammi's little brother Hal stood in my doorway, the twins behind him. Hal's face was pale where the skin showed through the tear smears and the dirt. His eyes were huge. Cammi sat up and opened her arms. Hal ran to her and hugged her and Beast.

"Come on, kids." Mom's voice floated up the steps. "Come get some breakfast. Then we'll go through the suitcases and see what we've got for all of you to wear."

After we ate and got cleaned up, Cammi and I wandered over to her house. She cried quietly as we stood on the sidewalk and stared. Half the house, the half near the garage, looked terrible. The windows were broken. Part of the roof was gone, and what was left had a hole hacked in it. The front door hung crookedly, half torn off its hinges. Black soot covered the brick front and the white siding. Some of the shrubs planted along the front of the house were broken, and the lawn looked more like a mud field than grass. The other half of the house looked very dirty but otherwise fine.

"The firemen went in the front door and stopped the fire before it got to the bedrooms," Cammi said. She pointed to the far end of the house. "That's my room."

"Then maybe your dolls will be all right?"

Tears filled her eyes again and she shrugged. "Maybe," she whispered. She took a couple of deep breaths while I studied the devastated garage.

"Bugs!" Cammi screamed suddenly. "Come here, Bugs!" She began clapping the way animal people do.

I jumped and grabbed my ear. "Ouch, Cammi! I'm probably deaf for life."

She looked at me as I shook my head to get rid of the ringing, and she almost smiled as she said, "Sorry."

"Missing something, kid?"

We both spun around in surprise. It was the tall guy named Tree, and he still had his camera around his neck. Instinctively Cammi and I moved closer to each other and farther from him. He didn't seem to notice. He just grinned widely.

"Looks pretty well messed up, doesn't it?" he

said happily. "Here, let me take your picture." And before we knew it, he had clicked several times.

"Who's Bugs?" he asked when he lowered his camera.

"My cat," Cammi whispered.

"Got killed, huh?" Tree asked with interest.

"No," said Cammi. "No. He just got scared and ran away."

"Oh," said Tree. "Sure."

"Come on, Cammi." I said. "Let's go back to my house. Your mom and dad will be there any minute."

I wanted to get away from Tree. He was my third East Edge person, and he'd put my opinion of the town on a skid it might never recover from. I grabbed Cammi by the arm and dragged her across the street just as the moving van pulled up to our house.

Please, God, isn't there some way you can get me back to Indiana? I thought of snobby Brooke. I looked at weepy Cammi. Then I glanced back over my shoulder at Tree. I shivered. *Please, God! I hate it here!*

I spent the better part of the day watching people go back and forth between our house and the Restons'. It seemed as though everyone in East Edge dropped by to see the fire damage, offer to help, and then come over to meet the new minister. I got so tired of Mom saying, "And this is our daughter, Deanna. Dee, dear, this is Mrs. Somebody (or Mr. Whoever)." I smiled so many polite hellos I thought my cheeks would crack.

It didn't look at all like God was going to get me out of East Edge. Instead I felt like I was sinking into a bunch of quicksand, and I was going to be trapped forever. I also felt I'd scream if I got one more welcoming pat on the head. Finally I escaped to Cammi's so I wouldn't embarrass my parents by behaving the way I wanted to. I stood at her crooked front door and called her name. I could hear her feet going squish, squish on the carpet.

Cammi appeared at the door. In her arms she carried some dolls.

"Gosh, Cammi," I blurted, "you're smiling."

"Oh, Dee, you were right! They weren't ruined after all!" She stepped outside, and I saw the sorriest looking dolls I'd ever seen.

"The bedrooms are a mess from smoke, but nothing in them got wet or burned," she said. "Here, hold these while I get some more." She dumped three smelly, dirty dolls in my arms and started back for more.

"You know, these dolls smell," I said, wrinkling my nose. "Maybe you should just toss them."

Cammi's eyes grew wide. "Never! These are my babies!" And she went back into the burnt house to rescue some more.

I stood there feeling like a terrible mother forced to cuddle her dirty, smelly children against her will. While I waited, a tall—make that a very tall—girl came up the walk.

"Hi," she said. "I'm Shannon."

I smiled over my doll-filled arms, hoping I didn't look as stupid as I felt. "I'm Dee."

Shannon nodded. "The new pastor's kid."

"Do you play basketball?" I asked, then wished for a free hand to slap across my mouth before I said anything else I shouldn't. So she was tall, very tall. Like Mom always said, don't point out people's problems. They already know them.

But Shannon must have heard it before. She just shook her head. "Nah. I hate the game."

Cammi returned with four more dolls. Resting on top was a baby doll whose clothes and cloth body were black with soot. "Hi, Shannon. Here." She gave two of her four dolls to Shannon and studied the stained baby in the sunlight. "I hope we can clean her up."

"What if you can't?" Shannon asked.

"We'll take her to the doll hospital. They'll know what to do there."

I looked at the collection Cammi had brought out. "Are there many more?" I asked.

She nodded. "Lots."

"Then let's go to my house and get a box or two the movers are finished with. You can keep the dolls safe in them."

The three of us walked back to my house and talked Mom into emptying some boxes before she wanted to. We put the already rescued dolls in one and carried the others back to Cammi's. When we got there, two police cars were parked at the curb.

"What are they doing here?" I asked. "Something must be wrong!"

Cammi shook her head. "They're just checking things out, I guess." A young policeman with glasses held the crooked door open for another officer and Cammi's mom. Mr. Reston stood in the doorway and solemnly shook hands with the officers. Mrs. Reston tried to smile at them, and they each gave her a big hug.

I blinked. Maybe the people in East Edge weren't very friendly, but the cops sure were. They stopped and hugged Cammi, too.

"Sorry, kid," said the one with glasses.

"Thanks, Mr. Ryan."

We stood on the curb and watched them drive away.

"My mom's a police officer," Cammi explained, noticing my amazement. "They're her friends."

I looked at Cammi with interest. I'd never known anyone whose mother was a cop. The father of one of the guys in my class in Indiana was a policeman, but nobody's mother.

I followed Cammi and Shannon up the walk. We left the boxes on the porch and went into the house. What a mess!

There was a line around the walls about two feet from the ceiling. Above the line everything was burned black, black, black. Below it, the walls looked fine.

The ceiling had collapsed—from the weight of the water, Mr. Reston told me later—and chunks of white plaster were all over. Streamers of pink fiberglass insulation hung down from the rafters, some reaching all the way to the floor, some floating free, moving whenever anyone walked close.

The tops of all the furniture were covered with slimy, black soot, but, surprisingly, the bottoms looked clean.

The rug was squishy and black, and I kept wondering what color it used to be. A matted down path showed where the firemen had gone in and out the front door and stood to keep the fire from the bedrooms.

Several plants in the big, blown out front window were wilted and black. They had boiled to death, as had the fish floating belly up in the black water of the fish tank in the corner.

And over everything was the smell . . . dark, nasty, and terrible.

"Where are you going to live, Cammi?" I asked. "You certainly can't live in here."

"I heard Mr. Picardy—he's our insurance man— tell Mom and Dad that he's rented a two-bedroom apartment for us at Green Springs. We're supposed to live there until the house gets fixed."

Shannon nodded. "Green Springs is nice."

"Where's Green Springs?" I asked.

"Near Dad's school," Cammi said.

"Your father's a teacher?"

Cammi nodded. "He's principal of East Edge High School."

We reached Cammi's room. I could tell it must have been pretty before the fire. Now the rose flowered bedspread and curtains and the rosy rug were all peppered with that terrible black soot. I reached out and wrote "Dee" in the soot on her bureau.

A big display cabinet full of dolls stood in the corner of the room farthest from the garage, unhurt.

"The better dolls live in that case and were protected," Cammi said. "The more ordinary ones were just sitting around."

Shannon picked up a Raggedy Ann from the floor and shook it. Soot billowed from Ann's red yarn hair and her apron.

"That's Barbie," I said, pointing to the cabinet. "Why's she in there? There are millions of Barbies."

"She's one of the original Barbies, and she's wearing her original outfit," Cammi said. "You'd never believe how much money she's worth."

But I forgot about Barbie. I lifted out a large, blond doll in an old fashioned, full blue dress with lots of lace on it and ruffled pantaloons underneath. The doll's little feet were thrust into patent leather slippers, and a big hat with blue, yellow, and cream ribbons hung from her wrist. Her cheeks were a delicate pink, and her eyes were the same blue as her dress.

Even I had to admit she was a pretty impressive looking doll. "She's beautiful!"

Cammi looked proud, like a new mother bringing her baby to the church nursery for the first time. "She's a boudoir doll from the 1930s."

"What's boudoir mean?" I ran a finger over the shiny golden curls.

"Bedroom," Cammi said. "You were supposed to put her on your bed as decoration. You don't play with her; you look at her. My grandfather gave her to my grandmother when they got engaged in 1947. Her name's Pansy because the blue in her dress is like the blue in pansies."

I nodded and held Pansy very carefully.

Suddenly Cammi got all teary. She sat down on her bed, then jumped right up with a black seat. She couldn't decide whether to dry her eyes or brush off her shorts, so she just stood there. "I don't want to go to Green Springs. What if Bugs comes home and no one's here?"

I took a deep breath. Dolls and now a cat. "I guess I could look out for him," I said.

"But he doesn't know you." She picked up an armful of her ordinary dolls. "He won't come to you. And they won't let us take Beast to Green Springs, either. Mr. Picardy says we should just chain him out back here by the woods."

"Would that be too bad? The twins and I could come and feed him and make sure he has water."

"But he's old, Dee. He can't hear real well anymore, and he bumps into things sometimes. He'll think we've deserted him or something."

We carried the dolls out to the boxes and put them carefully inside. There were still several empty boxes, which was a good thing because there were lots of dolls waiting in Cammi's room.

"This is a really old doll," I said, looking at the painted head of the one I had in my hands. Her features were Oriental, her dark hair piled high with fancy pins holding it in place, and she wore a beautiful red and gold robe with a gold sash around her waist.

Cammi nodded. "Very old. You should see the ones my grandmother has!"

"Does your mom like dolls, too?" Shannon asked as we went back inside for another load.

"Not too much. She likes hobbies that accomplish something, she says, like knitting."

I could understand that.

So could Shannon. "My mom likes to make stuff with dried flowers. We've always got bunches of weeds hanging upside down from the pipes in the cellar for her wreaths and all. I keep bumping into them." She looked at me. "My mom's quite small. I take after my father."

When we came out with the last load of dolls, I was afraid we wouldn't have room in the boxes, but they all fit better than I had expected.

It took us three trips, but we carried every box and doll from Cammi's porch to my room. Then we very carefully took them out and arranged them on the floor. Shannon took special care with Raggedy Ann.

I stood in the middle of the room and looked at all the smiling faces.

"How do you live with them staring at you all the time?" I asked.

Cammi actually giggled. "They're my friends," she said. "They don't stare at me because they know it's impolite."

Great. Just my luck to have a room full of dolls that only stared at me.

"Where's Pansy?" I asked, spinning in a circle. "I think she's so pretty."

We looked around the room, but the figure with long blond curls and the blue gown and straw hat wasn't there. Neither was Barbie or the lovely Oriental doll.

They had disappeared.

"Dee." Mom's voice floated up the stairs as Cammi, Shannon, and I stared at each other.

"Maybe we left a box at Cammi's," Shannon said.

I shook my head. "There wasn't anything left on the porch. I looked around."

We looked somberly at the empty boxes.

"We had my dolls. Then we didn't. What happened to them?" Cammi was ready to cry again.

"Could someone have taken them?" My voice was full of doubt.

"Who? When?" Cammi was as confused as I was, and tears began sliding down her cheeks.

"Dee," Mom called again. "Come to the top of the stairs, if you please."

I did as she asked. When she says "If you please," it means "You'd better do what I'm asking and right this minute!"

"Mom, some of Cammi's dolls are missing."

"That's not surprising, considering," she said.

"No, they're not missing in the fire. They're missing since we brought them out of the house. I even carried two of them out myself."

I heard a loud sniff in my left ear and realized Cammi had followed me out of my room.

"Maybe somebody stole them," she suggested.

"What?" Mom said in disbelief.

"When?" I said.

"Why?" Shannon said.

Cammi sniffed.

"I think you should go back and tell your mother, Cammi," said Mom. "She'll know what to do."

We girls looked at each other. All of us seemed to feel better at the idea.

"And now I've some news that will cheer you girls up," Mom said. "Mrs. Picardy just called to say Brooke has invited you and the boys to come out to their house this evening to go swimming."

"Oh, no!" I said before I thought. My mother believes you should only think and say nice things about people, and she gets distressed because I frequently say things I shouldn't.

Fortunately Mom misunderstood my reaction. She thought I was feeling bad for Cammi, not bad about Brooke.

"Don't worry, Dee," she said. "I spoke to Mrs. Reston, and she agrees with me that a swim is just what you all need, especially Cammi."

"Gosh," said Shannon, "I won't be able to go. Mom's picking me up any minute now. Isn't that a shame."

I looked at her. I'd never heard anyone sound less sad.

"And I don't have a suit," Cammi said quickly—so quickly I knew she felt the same way about Brooke that Shannon and I did. "It got all smoky-smelling in the fire. Besides, the last time I wore it, Brooke told me how tasteless it was." Cammi whispered the last sentence to Shannon and me.

"At least it's only your suit," Shannon whispered back. "She thinks my height is tasteless. Like I can do something about it."

"A bathing suit's no problem," said Mom, the great problem solver. "Dee's got two. You can just borrow the one you like most."

Cammi and I looked at each other. We knew when we were beaten.

Mom smiled up the stairs at us, happy for our wonderful plans. "Dinner will be ready in half an hour. Until then, Cammi, your mother would like to see you at your house."

I tagged along because I didn't want to be stared at by countless dolls while I waited for Cammi to return. Besides, we needed to tell Mrs. Reston about the missing dolls.

When we went out front, Shannon's mother had just pulled up in front of Cammi's.

Shannon grinned at us as she climbed into the front seat. "Have fun at Brooke's."

Cammi and I stood on her front walk and watched some men on the roof draping great sheets of heavy, bright blue plastic.

"What are they doing?" I asked.

"Covering the hole to protect the house from further damage until the insurance guys are done and the builders can fix it up."

We pulled the crooked door open and walked into a much darkened house.

"Cammi, if you have anything else you want to take with you, you need to get it now," said Mrs. Reston. "The men are almost finished boarding the windows, and we have to leave. We won't be back inside for a couple of days, maybe longer."

41

We walked to Cammi's room and she pulled out her bathing suit, a pink one-piece with a flouncy ruffled skirt edged in green. I thought it was kind of cute.

She smelled it and held it out to me to do the same. It smelled absolutely awful, just like everything else. She shrugged and tossed it onto the bed.

We wandered out to the woods behind Cammi's house and spent some time calling Bugs.

"Why's he named Bugs?" I asked. "Does he look like Bugs Bunny or something?"

"I found him about a year ago just over there." She pointed to a fallen tree that rested on a good sized rock. There was a small protected area beside the rock and under the trunk. "He was hiding there, trying to be invisible. I almost didn't see him because he's gray and sort of blended in with the shadow, and he was very little. I started playing with him, and he was so sweet. I took him home and told my father he had followed me." She grinned. "I don't think I fooled him, but he let me keep him anyway."

She bent down and looked in the little hiding place, but there was no cat there today. "Of course, when Bugs came home, Beast was already an old

42

man, just lying around all day. And Bugs loved him. He'd bat at Beast's tail, sleep on Beast's back, lick Beast's face. In other words, he bugged him all the time. So he became Bugs."

Her eyes filled with tears again. I was surprised she had any moisture left in her.

"I miss him," she whispered.

"He'll be all right," I said, hoping I was telling the truth. "You'll see. He'll come home, just like your dad said."

She nodded, but she didn't look convinced.

"Come on," I said. "Let's go get dinner."

She didn't move.

"Cammi." I touched her arm.

She looked at me with huge sad eyes.

"Oh, Bugs," she sobbed, "where are you?"

EAST EDGE
6
MYSTERIES

Dad drove Cammi, her little brother Hal, the twins and me to Brooke's.

"She's not going to be happy when she sees Doug didn't come," Cammi said. Doug was her older brother, the tall kid I'd seen at the fire holding Beast's leash. "He's in ninth grade, and she thinks he's wonderful. Though I could tell her a thing or two."

"You mean I won't do?" asked Hal, taking time out from his wrestling match with Mike and Phil in the back seat. "I'm your brother, too."

Cammi snorted.

"No, you won't do," said Phil. "Of course you won't do. But the three of us will. We're all in third grade, right? Three of us, third grade. Three times three equals nine, the same as Doug!"

Cammi snorted again. "She'll really buy that. Three wiggle worms!"

"Well, well," said Dad as he turned into Chartwell Chase. He always says "well, well" when he's surprised or doesn't know what to say. And Chartwell Chase was definitely a "well, well" sort of place. Every house in the development was a mansion.

"Are these guys we're going to see millionaires or something?" asked Mike. "Wow! Look at that car, will you? I bet it's a Rolls."

It was silver and a block long and had just pulled out of a driveway with a big wrought iron gate with curlicues on top.

"I don't know about millionaire, but Mr. and Mrs. Picardy have lots and lots of money," said Cammi.

After passing several very large, impressive houses, we pulled into the curving driveway of something Queen Elizabeth could live in. The front yard was a football field in size, but the turf was real and as green and lush as any yard I'd ever seen. All the shrubs and trees were just the right shape, and all the flowers were blooming their heads off.

But it was the house that overwhelmed me. It was huge! There were enough bricks in the thing to build the entire Yellow Brick Road, though these were more tan than yellow. And there were windows everywhere, big windows, little windows, curved windows, and windows that were really doors.

No wonder Brooke had looked up and down our street with her nose in the air.

Mr. Picardy came around the side of the house with a beautiful lady who looked as perfect as the house and lawn. Mrs. Picardy, of course.

"Come on out back, kids," he said. "The water's waiting."

We followed him in a long, single-file line like ducklings. I felt I should waddle, but decided waddling didn't go with Chartwell Chase. Only gliding, as done by elegant swans, would be welcome here.

"You're staying, too, aren't you, Pastor?" I heard Mrs. Picardy say to Dad as we walked through an opening in a hedge.

Dad must have said no, because Mrs. Picardy came around back alone, smiling brightly.

"So you're Deanna and Mike and Phil," she said. "I'm so glad you could come swim tonight.

And Cammi and Hal, I'm glad you came, too."

I had expected Mrs. Picardy to be stuck-up like Brooke, but she was very charming and pleasant. It was a nice surprise.

We were all standing, smiling brightly at each other, when Brooke appeared. She had on a black bathing suit like some slinky model might wear. She didn't look anywhere near as pleased to see all of us as her mother had been.

"Where's Doug?" she asked.

"Hi, Brooke. Good to see you, too," I said.

"He couldn't come," Cammi said.

"But he found his glasses," said Hal. "The fire didn't hurt them. Isn't that great?"

If somebody looked at me the way Brooke looked at Hal, I don't think I'd ever speak again. Hal just grinned.

"Now don't frown, Brooke," said her mother. She smiled lovingly at her daughter. "When you get to be my age, a frown like that will give you wrinkles."

The boys had been polite as long as they could stand. In a mad leap, they all jumped into the pool with its blue, blue water. I was fascinated by the bubbling spa in one corner of the shallow end.

Mrs. Picardy saw my interest. "Want to get in?"

She walked over and turned a switch, and suddenly the water leaped and jumped and frothed.

"Sit here," she directed. "This is my favorite spot."

I lowered myself into the bubbling water to a little seat. Immediately my back was pounded with a stream of water going round and round in a circle. And the water was much warmer than I expected.

I laughed out loud in surprise. "Come on, Cammi. This is great!"

We sat in the spa for about ten minutes. By then I was sweating and starting to feel lightheaded. We climbed out and sat on the edge of the regular pool, dangling our feet in the water. Brooke joined us without enthusiasm as her parents disappeared into the house.

"That suit's no improvement over the last one," she said to Cammi.

Cammi and I both looked at my red and navy striped suit she was wearing. I'm dark-haired and I buy bright-colored things, but Cammi's the kind of light blond who looks better in pastels. Still, the suit wasn't that bad. And even if it was, it was pretty rude to say so.

"Cammi's clothes got ruined in the fire, Brooke. That's my suit."

"Oh." Obviously she thought that explained a lot.

"Come on," I said to change the subject. "I'm still hot. Let's swim."

Cammi and I jumped in and began splashing around. I love the water, especially diving and swimming underwater. It was a couple of minutes before I realized Brooke wasn't in the pool with us.

"Aren't you coming in?" I asked.

"I don't like to get wet," she answered in that snobby voice of hers. She gently patted her hair, blown dry, curled, and sprayed into what she obviously thought was a beautiful hair-do. It reminded me of a cartoon of someone who had stuck her finger in an electrical socket.

"Okay," I said and dived. I came up spitting and spouting and happy.

I was floating on my back, something I love to do, when I saw we had another guest at our swimming party. A little white-haired man with a cane came through the break in the hedge.

"Hi, Brooke!" he called, waving.

"Oh, no," she muttered. "It's Mr. Maples!"

"Who's Mr. Maples?" I asked.

"He lives next door, and he comes to visit us all the time because he's lonely. His family's too busy spending his money to visit him, and his butler's as old as him and too deaf to talk. So Mr. Maples comes here to talk."

"That's bad?"

Brooke looked at me like I was too dumb to know bad when I heard it.

"You're looking lovely tonight, my dear," the old man said pleasantly to Brooke. He walked carefully to the edge of the pool, obviously afraid of slipping in the water we had splashed all over the place.

"And who are these delightful young people?" He pointed his cane at us. He had a very friendly smile.

Brooke, with her usual fine manners, said nothing.

I smiled back at the old man and introduced all of us. Even the little boys stopped chasing each other long enough to behave better than Brooke.

"You all sounded like you were having such fun that I just had to come say hello. I live alone, you see, except for Mr. Jones, my deaf and cantankerous old butler. After looking at his grumpy face all day, it gives me great pleasure to speak with lovely people such as yourselves."

He smiled and gave a little goodbye bow. Carefully he walked back through the break in the

50

hedge. He turned just before he disappeared and gave us a final wave.

Cammi and I waved back. Brooke snorted.

"Why don't you like him?" I asked. "He seems very nice."

"He's a pain."

"But he's lonely," said Cammi.

"He's a pain."

I shook my head and dived. I surfaced on the other side of the pool and looked back at Brooke. Was it hard to be so unfailingly nasty?

Just then the three boys decided to be cannon balls. Hal jumped with a great shout, and a respectable splash followed. We all cheered — except Brooke, of course.

Then Phil and Mike jumped in at the same time, and a great fountain gushed up—all over Brooke.

She jumped up and screamed. "Look what you did! Look what you did! You got me wet! You little jerks! You got me wet!"

She grabbed a towel and began patting herself dry as though she might start to dissolve any second. On one half of her head her hair looked the way she planned, still curly and dry. On the other side it was all wet and stringy—probably just like mine.

I had to work not to laugh, and I was afraid to look at Cammi.

The twins were completely unaware of what they'd done, having been underwater when Brooke told them off. So she told them again when they surfaced.

And then I told her.

My mom calls it "circling the wagons." The old pioneers may have argued among themselves, but when the Indians attacked, they circled the wagons and protected each other. It was time for me to protect my brothers, though I don't think Mom would have liked the way I did it.

"You are the snippiest, nastiest, most stuck-up person I've ever met!" I yelled. And that was just the beginning.

I don't know who was more surprised at my outburst, me or Brooke. I just knew it was a good thing my mother couldn't hear me. I also knew I should apologize, but I couldn't make myself do it.

When Mr. and Mrs. Picardy came outside a few minutes later with sodas and popcorn, they found a very quiet and unsmiling group.

East Edge just kept getting worse all the time.

I woke up Monday morning all scrunched up on one side of my bed, my feet hanging over the edge. I was sweating like crazy.

I looked down at the reason for my discomfort, Beast. He had climbed on my bed while I slept and had made himself comfortable.

"So glad you feel at home," I said.

He raised his huge head and grinned.

Cammi's and my parents had decided to let Beast stay with us rather than tie him behind the Restons' house. Cammi and Hal standing there in tears had probably had something to do with the arrangement. If Bugs ever showed up, he was to be our house guest, too.

Cammi and Hal would come over and spend

each day with us, but they would go home to Green Springs each night. Mrs. Reston felt it was important for the family to be together as much as possible.

Beast stood up and began relocating himself, and I thought my bed would collapse. Before I knew it, his head was on the pillow beside mine, and he kissed me. I wouldn't have to wash my face this morning.

I rolled onto my back and stared at the teddy bears. Sometime during the past couple of days they had started to look cute to me. I'd better watch it or I might start to like East Edge.

Yesterday had been our first day at Dad's new church. I went with a chip on my shoulder because I wanted to be in Indiana with Allison and Mandy, but I had to admit people were nice. No one patted me on the head.

The Sunday school class for my age was larger than I expected, and I was glad to see Shannon again. Our teacher was a young nurse named Gail.

"We all love Gail," Cammi had told me, but I hadn't believed her. I was expecting a Pennsylvania version of Mrs. Woodstone, sort of old and sour.

But Gail was very impressive. She liked to laugh, and she was an interesting teacher. I had the most radical thought as I listened to her: I might learn to enjoy Sunday school.

Not that I hated it or anything. I didn't. I'd gone all my life. Pastors' kids don't have a choice. Mostly, I'd had fun at church and church things. I certainly loved Jesus and I wanted to be a good Christian. The only thing that got in my way was me. And the move to East Edge.

Gail made a big thing over my joining the class. "We're very glad you're here, Dee," she said. "I know moving can be hard. When circumstances change, it seems bad, but God lives here in East Edge, too, and He never changes."

She smiled warmly at me. I smiled back and wondered if she'd been talking to my father.

"And, Cammi, I'm so thankful you're all right!"

All the girls nodded, and Cammi looked ready to cry again.

"Tuesday afternoon," said Gail, "we'll have a swim party at Brooke's. It'll be a welcome party for Dee and a shower for Cammi. That means we'll have fun and get to know Dee, and we'll bring a gift for Cammi since she lost all her belongings in the fire."

Sounded good to me. I looked at Brooke and wondered how she felt about us all coming. I also wondered if she ever actually got in her pool.

She sat across the circle from me and looked every inch the rich lady. Most of us had on cool, sleeveless knit dresses or, in a couple of cases, slacks, and we wore sandals and had bare legs.

Not Brooke. She wore a short navy skirt and a navy and white checked top. She had on white stockings and patent leather shoes, and she sat with her knees together—just the way Mom always told me I should sit. Lady Brooke didn't even look hot, while I felt slick with sweat.

"I'm really worried about Bugs," Cammi told Gail and the class. She had to clear her throat so she wouldn't cry. "We haven't seen him since the fire. Dee and I have gone down in the woods several times to look for him, but we haven't seen him. Would you pray for him?"

"I sure will," said Gail, and she did right then and there. I don't think old Mrs. Woodstone would have prayed for an animal, but Gail knew how important Bugs was to Cammi.

I smiled at Gail and realized I'd finally met someone in East Edge I actually liked! If I pulled my hair back on the sides with combs like she did, would I look as nice? After all, we both had lots of dark hair.

I reached up and sort of pushed one side of my hair back and tucked it behind my ear. It stayed about ten seconds before it bounced back the way it had been. Don't let anyone fool you. Naturally curly hair is a curse.

Dad preached a good sermon that morning. I know he and Mom had been praying that he do well, because they felt it was important for him to be good his first Sunday.

"First impressions are hard to erase, Sandy," Dad said to Mom. "So keep praying."

So she did and he did. And the new congregation seemed happy.

But it was after church that I learned about a wonderful and special thing. I was standing by the side door of the church, waiting for Mom and Dad so I could go home and get some food.

"Dee!" Cammi ran over to me with a black girl, Alysha, who had also been in our class. Both Cammi and Alysha were vibrating with excitement.

"Guess what?" Cammi asked, but she didn't wait for an answer. "My parents' Sunday school class took an offering for us because of the fire, and they collected a thousand dollars!"

Cammi was grinning as hard as she had been

crying when I first met her. It suddenly dawned on me that she was probably a very pleasant person when her house wasn't in ruins and she wasn't suffering from crying fits every fifteen minutes.

"Isn't that great?" Alysha said, dancing around like a boxer. Suddenly she did about six cartwheels in a row. Legs and skirts flashed, but she moved so fast, nothing embarrassing showed.

"She's a gymnast," explained Cammi as Alysha bounced back to us.

"Is she always this hyper?"

"Always. It drives the teachers crazy. They can never figure out where to put her because she distracts everybody around her. But she's a straight A student and they can't help but like her."

I looked into Alysha's smiling face and couldn't help smiling back. I could use some fun.

Suddenly five little black boys came charging around the corner of the building.

"Alysha! Alysha!" they all yelled.

"Get lost!" she yelled back happily. "We're celebrating!"

"Mom wants you," yelled one.

"Are they all your brothers?" I asked, trying to imagine living with five little brothers. I found two more than enough.

Alysha shook her head. "If they were, I'd have to take karate instead of gymnastics. Just two are mine, Damon and Thetis. The rest are cousins."

"It's not Mom that wants you," said one little guy who bounced like Alysha. "It's Dad. He's hungry and wants to go home. I'm hungry and want to go home."

"That's Thetis," Alysha said. "He's four. Damon's the one with the blue plaid shirt. He's seven. Like his shirt? I gave it to him yesterday for his birthday."

"Very nice," I said, slightly stunned by all the energy they possessed. Not one of them stood still."

"What are you celebrating?" asked Damon as he swayed from side to side.

"Cammi got a thousand dollars to help her get over the fire!" Alysha did a back flip.

"A thousand dollars!" Little Thetis's eyes were wide, and he actually jumped up and down. "That's almost a million! Are you lucky, Cammi!"

"It's not my money, Thetis," Cammi said. "It's for my family."

Thetis looked disappointed. "Well," he said as he grabbed Alysha's hand and pulled her away, "it's still nice."

"A thousand dollars!" I said later to Mom and

Dad. "Isn't that great?"

"I saw people giving Mrs. Reston bags of clothes for the kids," Mom said. "And the women have made a schedule for sending dinner to the family each night so she can concentrate on all the work the fire has created."

"A Mr. Wright manages a big store in the mall, and he gave the Restons bedding and towels," Dad said. "I find it very encouraging to come to a church this caring!"

"I wonder what I can do to help," I said.

"You're helping by keeping the dolls," said Mom.

The dolls. They sat around my walls and stared at me and made my room smell just like a fireplace.

"But that's not like actually doing something. That's more *not* doing something, like not throwing them out. I want to *do* something."

"You're keeping Beast," said Dad.

"Do we have a choice?" I replied. "Cammi'd never stop crying if Beast were tied behind her house. No, I want to *do* something."

But I had no idea what it could be. I knew a professional cleaning service was coming to the Restons' to clean things up, and a contractor was going to make the place livable. I couldn't do those things any way.

I lay next to Beast and sweated and stared at my teddy bears and waited to be inspired. Nothing happened except that Beast kissed me again.

Cammi and I sat on the front steps in the morning sunshine.

"Our vacation should have started Saturday," she said, a faraway look in her eyes. "We were supposed to go to the shore for two weeks. Ocean City, New Jersey." She sighed. "I love Ocean City. I should be riding my raft or diving under the waves or sitting on the beach. Instead, here I am in East Edge."

"I know just how you feel," I said. "I'm not so wild about East Edge, either."

Neither of us said anything for a few minutes. We stared at a crack in the sidewalk and watched some very tiny ants parade from their house to a crumb of cookie and back.

Then, "One of my dolls is an Ocean City doll," Cammi said. "It's a Mary Hoyer doll. At least that's what we call it. When Mom was a little girl, there was this shop on the boardwalk that had wonderful dolls. Grandmom wanted to buy Mom a Madame Alexander doll, but she couldn't afford it, so she bought Mom one of the Mary Hoyer dolls. Then she bought a new costume for the doll every year. I think Grandmom hoped Mom would like the doll, but she never did."

Cammi sniffed and blinked, and I could see the waterfall was only nanoseconds away. "I love that doll, but the store's not there anymore, and I can't buy any more outfits." She leaned over and rested her forehead on her knees as if in pain.

"Did you tell your mom about Pansy and Barbie and the Oriental doll?" I asked, hoping to distract her from Mary Hoyer.

Cammi nodded and sniffed and sighed, all at the same time. "She said we'd probably never see them again. . . . "

So much for preventing the tears.

"Was she mad?"

"My mom?" Cammi shook her head. "Of course not. She was very nice. But I have to tell Grandmom I lost the dolls."

More tears, and Cammi sniffed again. "Do you have a tissue? Grandmom's going to be so upset."

"Hey, she'll understand," I said. "Grandmothers are like that."

"Maybe." She sniffed a couple of times.

We watched the ants again. The crumb was almost all gone.

"Come on," I said. "We'll go get a tissue and then look for Bugs."

We walked across the street and stared at the bedraggled house.

"Mom and Dad have to pick out shingles this morning so the roof can be repaired," Cammi said. "And siding and shutters and new doors. Then they have to pick out carpeting and furniture and wallpaper and paint."

"Won't they pick out the same as you had?"

"Most of the time, I think. But Mom wants to get the living room stuff in different colors." Cammi grinned weakly. "Dad keeps teasing her that it would have been easier just to buy new things than to burn the house down. He wouldn't have complained that much."

"Cammi!" A girl was running and waving at us from down at the corner. "Cammi!"

But Cammi didn't seem to hear. "I wish Mom

would stop her nervous shaking," she said. "And I keep waking up, thinking I hear the smoke alarm. Then I can't get back to sleep."

I looked at her and for the first time noticed the dark circles under her eyes. Had they been there all along and I was too dumb to see them?

Dear God, I thought again, *I want to do something. Please give me an idea.*

"Cammi!" The girl was almost to us. "Cammi!" Finally Cammi heard her.

"Bethany! How was Rickett's Glen?"

"Cammi, what happened?" The girl stared open-mouthed at the house. "I was coming to feed Beast and Bugs while you're in Ocean City. But you're here. What happened?"

"Fire. Friday night."

"No one was hurt, were they?"

"We're all okay."

"How did it start?"

"We don't know yet. But it started in the garage."

"I can tell that just by looking. No roof." She kept shaking her head in disbelief. "Where are you living?"

"Green Springs. In a two-bedroom apartment."

"So who gets the living room for sleeping?"

"Doug. Hal and I are sharing a bedroom. It's weird sleeping with a little brother. He groans in his sleep. When did you get home?"

"Last night about midnight. Dad insisted on hiking down the Falls Trail again before we left. We stopped for pizza in Tamaqua on the way home."

"Our families camp together sometimes," Cammi said, remembering me. "This is Bethany Stoller. She lives just around the corner. And this is Dee," she said to Bethany.

"The new pastor's daughter!" Bethany said.

I nodded. When other kids got introduced, people never said, "The new taxi driver's kid!" or "The new insurance man's kid." It was just "The new pastor's daughter."

But I knew Bethany didn't mean anything by it. Her smile and braces that sparkled in the sun proved that.

She was an interesting looking person. Aside from the braces, her face was broken out. I tried to think of anyone I knew in the sixth grade who had zits, and I couldn't remember anyone. Did it mean she was more mature than the rest of us? It might, because she had the beginnings of a chest, too.

"Bugs is missing," Cammi said. "He ran off

during the fire. Dee and I have looked and looked for him, but we haven't found him yet."

The three of us went through the woods calling his name, but we got no response. The one nice part of hunting him was that it was cooler in the woods that in the record-breaking sun. What a good week it would have been to be in Ocean City.

"Let's go wash some dolls' clothes," Cammi suggested when it became obvious that Bugs wasn't around.

"So your little family survived," Bethany said. "I was afraid to ask."

"They're pretty dirty and smelly," I said. "They're now living in my bedroom, and they make it smell like a fireplace."

We wandered out of the woods and across the Restons' backyard.

"Oh, look!" said Bethany. "Your picnic table!"

We walked over to a pile of reddish wood. I only knew it was a picnic table because Bethany had said it was.

"What a mess!" I kicked at a couple of loose pieces.

"Dad kept saying he was going to paint it," Cammi said. She shrugged. "Well, he doesn't have to now."

"It doesn't look burned, does it?" I said.

Bethany squinted up at the roof. "Something must have fallen on it."

We wandered back to my house and spent a couple of boring hours washing dolls and dolls' clothes. At least I thought it was boring. Cammi loved it, and Bethany didn't seem to mind.

The dolls with ceramic or plastic heads and bodies cleaned up well. The fabric ones didn't. The soot didn't want to budge, and the smell stuck no matter what we did. Most of the clothing kept that terrible scorched odor, too, and so did the dolls' hair.

Cammi picked up the Mary Hoyer doll that had been her mother's. "Smell," she said, and stuck the doll's hair in my face.

"Not too bad," I said. "It must have been in the cabinet."

Cammi nodded.

"How many were protected?" I asked.

"Ten, including this Cabbage Patch one." Cammi adjusted its yarn hair. "The ones that weren't in the cabinet aren't very valuable, but I love them because they're mine."

We sat the homely Cabbage Patch doll named Chrissy on the kitchen table beside the elegant Mary Hoyer doll.

"I wish I knew where those missing dolls were," Cammi said. "I worry about them. What if they get hurt?"

"They're not real, Cammi," I said.

She nodded. "Yes, they are. Anybody who loves dolls knows that."

"What missing dolls?" Bethany asked.

We explained the theft to her as we took the cleaned dolls back up to my room, where they resumed their rude staring. About half of them were naked because their clothes were either ruined or needed ironing, and I had to fight the feeling that they were embarrassed and/or cold.

They are not real, I kept telling myself. They are not real. I think Bethany felt weird around them, too, because she seemed happy to leave for dinner.

Cammi's family stayed to eat with us, and while the parents talked, she and I went for another Bugs hunt. Doug and Hal and the twins came with us.

Even if Bugs wanted to come home, I think our noise level would have scared him off. But we had fun, and Cammi actually laughed when Doug jumped out from behind a big tree and scared the little boys so badly they sputtered.

On the way back to our house, Cammi and I

showed the guys the broken picnic table.

"At least Dad won't have to paint it now," Cammi said.

"What do you think broke it?" asked Hal. "It must have been something pretty big to break it up like this." His little-kid eyes were huge.

Doug stared at the table for several minutes, looking grim. "It wasn't a some*thing* that did this," he said. "It was a some*one*. This table was deliberately chopped into pieces."

Doug looked at the boys.

"Go get the parents," he said. His voice was so commanding that the boys never even blinked. They just took off.

I stared at the shattered picnic table. Now that Doug had said it had been destroyed on purpose, I could see what he meant. There were marks on the wood from an ax, neat marks that could never have come from something heavy falling on it. And the ground all around was littered with lots of little wood chips like those Dad gets when he chops fireplace wood.

The kids came back with Mom and Dad and Mr. and Mrs. Reston. We all stood in a semicircle around the sad pile of wood and stared.

"The third thing," said Mrs. Reston. She looked at Mr. Reston as she spoke, and she seemed very upset.

"What third thing?" asked Hal.

"Nothing," said his mother, obviously regretting what she had said. But it was an adult "nothing" that really meant there was a big something, but nothing they were going to tell us kids.

"Go collect your stuff at the Dennings'," Mr. Reston said to Hal and Cammi. "We have to get home."

"You kids go help," Mom said to us. "And you may all have a Popsicle. Just please close the freezer door this time."

All three of the little guys raced for our house. Cammi started to leave, but I put my hand on her arm. I had long ago learned that if I just hung around adults and kept quiet, I would learn all kinds of things. I pulled her to the ground, and we sat in the twilight, leaning against the house, listening.

"I think there may be four things, Dad, not three," said Doug. He pushed his glasses back on his nose and stuffed his hands in his pockets. "I can't find my bike."

Mrs. Reston punched the air in anger and

distress. But she wasn't mad at Doug. She was mad at some unknown person. "Where did you last have it?"

"I left it parked against the back of the house behind the lilac bush last night when we went to Green Springs. Nobody should have known it was there. It couldn't be seen. But it wasn't there when I came for it this morning. I had to walk to Tim's."

I looked at the great lilac bush at the corner of the house where Doug's bedroom was. The leaves were so thick that I couldn't see the house through them. Anyone who found a bike there was not just passing by but looking around to make trouble.

"Did you see anybody who doesn't belong in the neighborhood?" Mrs. Reston asked.

"Just some guy in the distance riding a bike."

"Yours?"

Doug shook his head. "I don't know. When I saw him, I didn't know my bike was missing. He was too far away, anyway."

Mrs. Reston nodded. I don't think she had really expected Doug to have any information.

"You've had four things stolen since the fire?" Dad asked, obviously surprised and distressed.

Mr. Reston shook his head. "Four very strange things total, one of which was the fire."

I felt Cammi jump at her father's words, and I looked from him to Mrs. Reston and back.

"Your fire was arson?" asked Dad.

Mrs. Reston nodded, looking very tired. "We knew unofficially from the beginning, but we just got the official word today. We could see the V pattern on the garage wall near the window—a black pattern that indicates the quick flash of an incendiary device. It can't be hidden."

"And," said Mr. Reston, "the window near the V pattern was broken inwards, the obvious point of entry to plant the bomb. All the windows broken by the fire exploded outwards."

I remembered all the pieces of glass shining in the sun the first morning. The yard had been covered with them. They were all picked up now, along with all the other debris. I wondered briefly who had done that awful job.

"There was also the remnant of a plastic gallon container in the garage," Mr. Reston said. "It was probably filled with gas, and when the original fire melted the plastic, the gas rushed out and fed the fire. That's one reason why so much was destroyed so quickly in the garage area."

"That's why the car exploded?" asked Doug. "Because of the extra gas?"

"Maybe," said Mrs. Reston. "Because the heat was so great, it may have broken the car windows sooner. If so, the flames rushed into the car more quickly, and it was the heat of the car burning that caused the car's gas tank to blow."

"But how did the fire begin originally?" Doug asked. "How did the bomb work?"

"The arsonist used a simple timing device made from an alarm clock. In fact, the wires remaining from the bomb were one of the proofs of arson."

I was really surprised that so much remained after a fire. I thought everything in the garage would have been burned up. But there were wires and plastic and V patterns left to be found.

Mrs. Reston must have been thinking like me. She said, "So many obvious indications of arson mean we're looking for an amateur, not a professional arsonist."

Mr. Reston put his arm around Mrs. Reston's shoulders. "The police are looking for someone Janie may have had a run-in with in the course of duty," he said.

I looked at Mrs. Reston and wondered what it was like to deal with people who could be so vengeful.

"Could it be a student that you upset, Henry?"

Mom was trying to look like she was used to discussing neighborhood crimes in the backyard.

Mr. Reston shrugged. "I guess it could be."

"So the bomb was attached to a clock," said Doug. "What was the actual bomb made of?"

I couldn't see Doug's face very clearly anymore because it was getting so dark, but I could hear how interested he was. I'd noticed that boys were like that, but I had to admit I was curious, too.

His father answered. "When the hands of the clock made a sixty-minute sweep of the dial and touched, they completed an electrical circuit and turned on a light bulb."

A light bulb? A light bulb had caused the fire?

He continued. "The glass of the light bulb had been separated from the base, filled part way with gas and reattached, probably with tape."

I was fascinated. Who would ever think of such a thing?

"When the light came on, the heat of the filament caused the gas vapors trapped inside the bulb to explode, ignite the liquid, and blow apart the bulb. The burning gas fell onto crumpled newspapers or something and took off."

"Fortunately the fire was set against the outside wall of the garage," said Mrs. Reston, "and by the time it burned through the door leading into the house, the smoke alarm had gone off."

"Thank God for smoke alarms," said Mom.

There was a moment's silence while we all thought about what might have happened if there had been no working smoke alarms.

"I don't think the person who did this wanted us to die from the fire or smoke," Mrs. Reston said. "I think he or she was interested in harassment. The petty thefts enforce that idea, too."

"You think it was the same person?" Dad asked.

"I'd hate to think that suddenly two people are after the Restons," said Mr. Reston. "Or three or four. I think it's one."

Later, lying in bed, I thought back to the conversation I had listened to. Arson. Somebody had deliberately set the Restons' house on fire. I couldn't believe anybody would do such a terrible thing. What if their smoke alarm hadn't been working? What if one of the Restons had died!

I shivered and rolled over. Beast, who was sleeping on the floor beside the bed, waiting for me to fall asleep so he could climb in, raised his head. I stroked him and felt comforted by his strength and warmth.

On Tuesday Cammi and I stood on the sidewalk with the twins and Hal and watched the roofers begin their job. They tore off all the remaining shingles off and tossed them to the ground. Then they patched the hole in the roof and laid the tar paper. By the time they actually got to the shingles, we were bored to death and long gone.

We made our usual sweep of the woods looking for Bugs and as usual didn't find him. We went to the grocery store with Mom and dropped some of the dolls at a doll repair shop in Downingtown. We ironed some of the dolls' clothes we had washed—or, I should say, we tried to iron them. Neither Cammi or I had ever done much ironing, and the clothes were so little, we kept ironing more wrinkles in than we could ever take out.

It was late in the afternoon when Mom drove us out to Brooke's for the Sunday school class swim party. Poor Cammi had to wear my red and blue striped suit again. I hoped Brooke wouldn't make any more cracks.

When we turned into Chartwell Chase, Mom didn't say "well, well" like Dad, but her eyes got big.

"I hate developments like this," she said. "They always make me jealous."

I grinned. Mom was about as jealous as a whale was skinny.

Gail and most of the class were there when we arrived. They were all in the pool splashing and diving and chasing each other. Cammi and I joined them while Mom and Mrs. Picardy made polite conversation. Brooke was nowhere in sight.

"Where's our perfect hostess?" I said a little too loudly and a lot too nastily. I meant for only Cammi to hear. Unfortunately Gail heard, too.

"She's at her piano lesson," Gail said, smiling. "She'll be here soon."

I nodded and dived to cool off my red face. I had to learn to be more tactful—or better yet, to keep my mouth closed completely.

By the time Brooke arrived, I was over the worst

of my embarrassment. I found myself trying to be extra nice to her to undo what Gail must think of me.

"Gosh, Brooke, it's nice to get to swim here again," I said.

She looked at me with one eyebrow raised. "Really?" she said, totally unimpressed by my goodwill.

I nodded. "This is such a lovely place."

She stared at me, then opened her mouth to say something, but we were interrupted by her mother.

"Dinner, girls," called Mrs. Picardy. "Take a place at one of the small round tables." She was behind a long table laden with food. A maid in an actual maid's uniform stood beside a large gas grill.

"Come on, Dee," said Cammi. She grabbed my hand and pulled me after her. We ended up at a table with Alysha, Bethany, and Shannon.

"I can't wait for one of Natalie's Bonzo Burgers," Shannon said. "I love to come here because Natalie's a great cook!"

"I love her homemade potato chips!" said Alysha.

I didn't even know you could make potato chips. I thought you had to buy them.

"Natalie's the maid?" I asked.

"And cook," said Bethany, adding unnecessarily, "the one in the uniform."

There were three tables of girls and one empty table on the flagstone patio. Mr. Picardy came out and took one of the three seats at the empty table. I figured Mrs. Picardy would take #2. Certainly Brooke wasn't expected to sit in #3?

I looked around. No, she was sitting with a table of girls. Somebody else was going to be #3. Just as my curiosity was about to get the best of me, I saw a familiar figure walk through the hedge.

"Mr. Maples," I said. "Hi."

"My dear girl, how nice to see you again. And your friend is back, too." He smiled at Cammi. "I'm afraid I don't remember your names, but your beautiful faces are inscribed on my heart."

Cammi and I giggled. What a nice man. We introduced ourselves again, as well as the girls at our table. He bowed to each of us like a cavalier in an old movie, then took a seat beside Mr. Picardy.

It didn't take me long to agree that Shannon was right. Natalie was a wonderful cook. I felt like a stuffed toy about to burst its seams when I finally finished. I licked the last of the lemon meringue off my fork, leaned back in my chair in a food-induced daze, and thought about nothing except maybe how good the Bonzo Burgers had been and how did you slice potatoes thin enough to make chips?

After a couple of minutes I tuned in on the conversation at the next table.

"I don't know, Mike," Mr. Maples was saying. "I keep asking my grandson Eddie to come clean out the cellar, but he never comes. I really need things straightened up down there, but I can't do it, and neither can Mr. Jones."

"Why not call a cleaning service of some kind?" Mr. Picardy suggested. "They could do whatever you needed."

Mr. Maples sighed. "I guess I'll have to. Mr. Jones suggests I do that, too."

Gosh, I wondered, did Mr. Jones have a first name? And did Mr. Maples ever use it?

"I'll be glad to give you the name of the company that does our spring cleaning," said Mr. Picardy. "Or you could just look in the Yellow Pages."

"Mike," said Mr. Maples, "do you call your father on the phone?"

"You mean, just to talk?"

"Yes."

"I try to call every week or two," Mr. Picardy said. "My mother calls me if I wait too long between calls, and she tells me about it." Mr. Picardy laughed. "My mother's a great lady."

"I never get phone calls from my sons." Mr. Maples voice was sad. "I've given up expecting visits, but you'd think one of the three could call once in a while."

"I expect they're just busy." I could tell from Mr. Picardy's voice that this was an old conversation.

"Busy spending my money," Mr. Maples said. "I ought to spend it all and beat them to it! In the old days, Mike, family stuck together and helped each other. Today, they just spend the old man's money."

"Mr. Maples," said Mr. Picardy, "you know how glad we are to have you be our family. With my parents living in Texas and Julie's in New York, we would be lonely indeed without you. Now let me get you another glass of iced tea. It's decaf."

I heard Mr. Picardy's chair scrape back. I waited until he was out of earshot, then I turned around. Mrs. Picardy had left the table, too, to serve desserts, so Mr. Maples was sitting alone.

"Mr. Maples," I said, trying to sound

trustworthy and businesslike. "I would like the job of cleaning out your cellar."

I was extremely nervous, and I could feel my heart pounding in my chest, trying to break out. I wondered if Mr. Maples could hear it thudding away.

He looked surprised by my request.

I slipped into Mr. Picardy's chair and leaned close. "I've been praying that God would show me something I could do for my friend Cammi. You see, her house burned down last week. I wanted to help in some way, but I couldn't figure out how. When I overheard you talking to Mr. Picardy, I suddenly knew. I could clean your cellar and then put the money I earn in the fund at church to help Cammi's family."

"Have you ever cleaned a cellar before?" Mr. Maples asked.

"No," I admitted. "But you have to start somewhere."

"And why should somewhere be my cellar?"

"Why shouldn't it?" I countered, smiling hopefully.

He didn't smile back. No wonder he had made a lot of money. I could see he was a hard businessman.

"I'm a hard worker. I'll do a good job. And you don't have to pay me if I don't do things well." I knew I'd better shut up. I was starting to sound desperate—which, of course, I was.

"You're offering me a money-back guarantee?" Mr. Maples asked, finally looking interested.

I nodded. "Exactly."

He looked at me from top to bottom. "How old are you?"

"Twelve next June." That was eleven months away, but maybe he wouldn't notice.

He looked down at his empty plate and was quiet for so long I was afraid he was going to tell me to get lost.

"Too bad my Eddie hasn't got your ambition," he said suddenly. "Too bad."

"Who's Eddie?" I asked.

"My grandson. He's lazy, lazy. Now me, I had ambition, just like you. That's how I made a fortune in electronics after World War II. My Ed, Eddie's dad, had it, too, but not Eddie." He nodded suddenly. "You come tomorrow at 9 o'clock. Mr. Jones will be looking for you."

I barely controlled a great urge to jump up and hug the old man. Instead I merely smiled and leaned close again. "Just don't tell anyone, okay? This is a secret between you and me. And my mother, who will have to bring me."

"Hiding your light under a bushel, eh?" He laughed. "Okay by me."

I turned back to my table, excited that I had found something I could *do* for Cammi.

A short time later she opened the gifts that the girls had brought for her. I felt cozy inside because I was going to give her an extra gift. She wouldn't know I was giving it, but I would and God would. That was enough.

The present I had brought for Cammi was the last one she opened. She pushed aside the tissue paper and pulled out a bathing suit, a pretty pink, yellow, and green floral one-piece with a matching ruffle scalloping across the top. She held it up for everyone to see.

"It's beautiful, Dee," she said. "Isn't it, Brooke?"

Brooke, of course, didn't reply.

"Go try it on," urged Shannon. Everybody else agreed.

When Cammi reappeared in her new suit, I could see the colors were just right for her. Even with her hair a wet mess, she looked cute.

We all took one last fling in the pool. Then one by one, parents started coming to collect daughters. In the confusion, I found myself standing beside Brooke.

I was all set to mind my manners and thank her, but she looked at me with disdain and spoke first.

"Don't think that just because there was a party to welcome you that we wanted you to come to East Edge. We didn't. And none of us wanted you to come here today, either. It should have been just us friends giving Cammi her party. Gail made us include you."

She looked over her shoulder to see who was near. Unfortunately no one was, so she continued. "You think Cammi likes you? Don't make me laugh! She just needs someone, that's all. Just wait. You'll see no one likes you."

She gave me one last what-rock-did-you-crawl-out-from-under look and walked away, smiling.

I felt like I'd been punched in the stomach. No one liked me? Cammi was just using me? Gail made them be nice to me?

All the dislike I'd ever had for East Edge and its residents flooded back, only larger.

God, please get me out of here!

When I rang the doorbell at Mr. Maples's house Wednesday morning, I was filled with so many mixed thoughts that I didn't know what was what.

I was glad that Cammi and her mother had picked today to shop for Cammi's room. And I was glad that Mr. Maples was willing to give me this job, my first real job for money.

But I couldn't forget what Brooke had said. Nobody wanted me in East Edge. And Cammi was just using me because I was handy, living across the street. Talk about a knife in the heart.

I hadn't said anything about Brooke's comments on the ride home from the party, either to Mom or Cammi. I hadn't known what to say. *Do you like me, Cammi? Does anybody like me?* Like I could really say that to anyone.

I went straight to my room as soon as I got home. Mom thought I was just tired. I climbed in bed and invited Beast to join me. I needed something warm to hug.

While I petted Beast, I cried, even though I kept telling myself I was being stupid. *You're just as bad as Cammi! Stop it!*

I was awake for a long time, staring at the dumb teddy bears. Just before I finally fell asleep, I remembered something Gail had said Sunday: God lives in East Edge, too, and He never changes.

Is it true, God? Are You still the same here even if the people aren't? If You are, will You help me? Can You help Cammi like me? And the other girls, too? Is it okay to ask something like that?

Now I stood at Mr. Maples's door listening to the doorbell chimes telling him and Mr. Jones that I was here.

I felt like getting back in the car and going home.

I felt like going to my room and staying there all day, not talking to anyone but Beast and the teddy bears.

I felt like screaming.

I felt like going back to Indiana.

I felt like being with Mandy and Allison.

And I felt absolutely terrible when I realized I had called my house here in East Edge "home."

Mr. Jones opened the door. I took a deep breath, waved to Mom, and stepped inside.

"Miss Denning," he said. "Mr. Maples is awaiting you in the sun room."

Awaiting! Mr Jones actually said awaiting!

He walked slowly and stiffly down the hall, obviously expecting me to follow him, so I did.

Mr. Maples had tea awaiting me in the sun room, and while I tried not to spill any on the floor or my lap, he told me what he would like me to do in his basement.

"I'm a collector, Dee," he said. "That's probably just a nice way of saying I'm a pack rat. I collect serious things like coins and stamps, and I keep all those books and supplies in my office just down the hall. I spend some time every day working with one collection or the other or both."

He fiddled with his hearing aid and leaned close like he was going to tell me a secret. If I got desperate, I thought, maybe Mr. Maples would be my best friend.

"When I go into my office to work on the stamps or coins," he said, "I turn my hearing aid off. That way I never get interrupted."

"What if your family tries to call?" I asked before I remembered I couldn't know about his family unless I had eavesdropped. And that wasn't a very good recommendation for me.

But Mr. Maples didn't seem to notice. "Don't worry. I have an answering machine. If they ever call, I'll know. Mostly I get calls from people trying to sell me things. I never call them back."

He paused to sip some tea and eat a donut hole.

"I love doughnut holes," he said. "They don't spill as much sugar on me as a doughnut does." He grinned. "I'm not very neat, you see. That's why I have Mr. Jones. He's a fussbudget and he keeps me neat."

Mr. Jones, who was just bringing another plate of doughnut holes, smiled sourly.

"Don't worry," Mr. Maples whispered. "He can't hear a thing. I can say whatever I like about him, and he'll never know." Mr. Maples laughed and took another doughnut hole.

"Can't Mr. Jones wear a hearing aid like you?" I asked.

"Wouldn't do him any good. They only work for certain kinds of deafness."

Another doughnut hole disappeared into his

mouth. I decided that another advantage to dough-nut holes is that they can be eaten fast enough not to slow you down when you're talking.

"I also collect useless things like paperweights," Mr. Maples said. He waved toward two shelves full of paperweights of all shapes and sizes. I set my cup down very carefully and walked over to them. A Liberty Bell, an Independence Hall, and a Betsy Ross flag with 1776 across it showed how close East Edge was to Philadelphia.

"That little man you just picked up is William Penn," Mr. Maples said. "Penn as in Pennsylvania."

But my favorites were the domed ones that whirled with snow when you shook them.

Mr. Maples seemed pleased that I liked them.

"That's my favorite," he said as I shook one that had a little farm complete with barn, silo, and the tiniest horses I'd ever seen. "It reminds me of the farm I grew up on."

I put it down very carefully and took my seat.

"Now for your business here," he said. "I also collect magazines. I started doing so by accident. One day I realized I had hundreds of issues of *National Geographic* and *Consumer Reports*, to say nothing of *Time* and *Forbes*. I realized Mrs. Maples had hundreds of *Ladies' Home Journal* and *Good*

Housekeeping magazines. So I started filing them like any good pack rat would. Then ten years ago we moved here, and almost immediately Mrs. Maples died."

He looked very sad for a minute. Then he shook himself like a dog, only he was getting rid of unhappy thoughts instead of water.

"I'm afraid the magazines never got unpacked. They sit in big boxes in the cellar. I would like you to unpack them and arrange them in the closet I had built for them when the house was built. It's a big closet, more like a small room, and it's full of shelves."

I nodded. I could do that.

"Mr. Jones will show you the way to the cellar. He and I don't go down there if we can avoid it. Our legs complain very strongly about stairs these days." He pushed a button.

"I thought Mr. Jones couldn't hear," I said.

"This isn't a buzzer; it's a light. Whenever it flashes, he knows I want him."

A minute later Mr. Jones entered the room.

"This way, Miss Denning," he said.

Mr. Maples put up his hand, and Mr. Jones stopped at the door.

"Dee," Mr. Maples said, "I'm going into my

office to work on my stamps. I'll be taking out my hearing aid. If you need me for any reason, just come right into the office and get me."

I nodded and followed Mr. Jones down a hall and through the kitchen—which was big enough to put three of our kitchens in—to a door. On the floor beside the door was a large box overflowing with magazines.

"Most of the magazines are downstairs," Mr. Jones said. "These are the most recent ones, and you'll have to take them down. Steps give me vertigo these days, and I avoid them whenever I can. Now if you will excuse me."

I was left alone to wonder what vertigo was.

I opened the cellar door and felt for the switch. When bright light flooded the stairwell, I felt better. I went cautiously down. The basement was very large and open, and it had small windows set high in the walls. There was a door to the outside against the back wall. Packing boxes were all around with odd items sitting on them or leaning against them or against the walls. I saw a large Christmas wreath, a toboggan, a bike, a set of barbells, an ax, a big saw, even a ratty looking fur coat.

No rooms had been divided off as they had in our cellar, where there were a furnace room, a workroom, and a playroom. The only enclosure in the whole place was the big closet along one of the walls. In front of the closet door were stacks of magazines and several big boxes.

I peered into the boxes. They were full of magazines, too, but the magazines were stuffed in metal holders that held a year's worth per holder. I pulled out a holder of *Good Housekeeping* and found the date 1954 on the front. I slid a magazine from the holder and opened it, and I nearly laughed out loud. The pictures and the clothes and the models and everything were so funny!

I reached into another packing box and took out a holder of *Ladies' Home Journal* dated 1949. I looked through it and decided the ads were the best and funniest parts. I also decided that I could spend all day reading these things and get no work done if I wasn't careful. I put the holders back in their boxes.

I stood for a minute looking at the boxes. It was very sad that they had never been emptied. Ten years of sitting there collecting dust. Of course, if they had been unpacked, the magazines would have still sat around collecting dust; they just would have done it from their shelves.

I turned to the piles of magazines. Here was a

mess. The different titles were mixed together, the dates were not in order, and most of them had never been read. I was surprised to find that Mr. Maples was still receiving *Ladies' Home Journal* and *Good Housekeeping* all this time after his wife died. I guessed that was so he could keep his collection up to date.

I went upstairs and got an armful of the magazines piled by the door and carried them down. Then another and another. Finally I picked up the last bunch and started down. By now my hands were filthy and my back hurt.

I was halfway down the steps when the biggest spider I'd ever seen crawled out of the pile in my arms. I screamed, threw everything in the air, lost my footing, and fell the last third of the way. I don't know where the spider fell, but I landed on my knees, scraping them slightly, and the magazines landed everywhere, bent and torn and a general mess.

I held my breath, waiting for Mr. Jones to throw open the door and ask what was the matter. Certainly I'd made enough noise to attract the entire neighborhood. Then he'd see what I'd done, tell Mr. Maples, and I'd lose my job. Then I wouldn't be able to help Cammi.

And, I realized, I wanted to help her whether she liked me or not. If God did live in East Edge and He never changed, then what He said didn't change, either. And He said we should help each other.

I waited on my hands and knees, but no door was thrown open, no one yelled, "What happened down there?"

Deafness, I decided, had certain advantages.

I picked myself up and tried to stop thinking about the spider. I hate spiders. They make my skin get all clammy and crawly. The rest of the time I worked, I kept looking for that big baby. I don't think I ever found him, but I came across plenty of his cousins. I hated every single one of them.

I began stacking the magazines by year, then arranging each year by months, then putting the years in order. By the time I was finished, I had sixty little piles sitting in a long line.

Sometimes I couldn't find a specific month, so I decided to write down the issues that were missing. Maybe Mr. Maples would want to buy them later.

I looked around for a pen or pencil and a piece of paper. There weren't many places to look. I worked my way slowly across the room, peering in boxes as I went, even feeling in the pockets of the old fur coat. There I found a ticket stub, a crumpled tissue and a button, but nothing to write with.

Not too far from the door that led to the outside, I flipped open a carton and found myself staring at a Barbie doll.

"Now whose can this be?" I said aloud as I lifted it out. Mr. Maples must have some granddaughters.

I looked back in the box and felt my heart begin to pound. I was staring at Pansy, her skirts all tumbled and her hat slightly crushed, but Pansy without a doubt. I picked her up, and underneath her was an Oriental doll in a red and gold robe.

Cammi's dolls? In Mr. Maples's basement? What was going on?

Certainly neither he nor Mr. Jones had taken them. First, they would have been noticed in the neighborhood. And second, they couldn't move fast enough to have gotten away before Cammi, Shannon, and I came out of Cammi's house with more dolls. And besides, the thought of either of those old gentlemen as a thief was ridiculous.

As I thought about the dolls, I looked around the cellar again. The bike!

I walked slowly toward it. How would I know if

it were Doug's? I didn't even know what color it had been.

Bingo! There was a name tag on the seat support that read "Property of Doug Reston." I guess when your mother's a cop, you label things more conscientiously than regular people.

I looked at the dolls in my hands, then at the bike. What should I do? Go upstairs and say, "Mr. Maples, you have stolen property in your basement"? Maybe I should call the police? Or Mrs. Reston? That was the same thing.

But Cammi's mom was shopping. I'd have to call the regular police.

I walked to the ax I'd seen leaning against the same box the fur coat was draped over. I studied it carefully, but there was nothing to indicate whether it had been used to chop up a picnic table—at least nothing I could see. But I remembered the evidence left from the fire. Maybe there were ways to check the ax, too.

I heard the cellar door open, and I spun around. "Mr. Jones!" I called.

But it wasn't the door at the top of the stairs. It was the door to the outside.

And it wasn't Mr. Jones. It was the tall, strange kid from the night of the fire. The kid named Tree.

I stared at Tree and he stared at me.

"What are you doing here?" he demanded. "And what are you doing with them?"

He reached out and grabbed Pansy and Barbie from me before I even realized what he was doing.

"Give them back!" I yelled. "They're not yours!"

I tried to snatch the dolls from him, but he just held them over his head and laughed.

"Mr. Jones!" I yelled. I made a break for the stairs. "Mr. Maples!"

I had taken about two steps when Tree grabbed me around the waist and picked me up. He clasped his hand across my mouth and pressed so hard tears came. Through the mist I could see Barbie and Pansy lying on the fur coat. At least he hadn't just dropped them.

"You shut up, girl," he hissed angrily in my ear. "You just shut up! Those deaf old men probably couldn't hear a fire siren in their bedrooms, but I'm not taking any chances."

I struggled, kicking and punching, trying to get away, but he was much too strong. He tucked me under his arm like a sack of feathers and carried me across the cellar toward the closet. By now his hand had slid from my mouth to my nose, too, and I could hardly breathe. I tried to pull his hand away, but it was like we were crazy-glued together.

For the first time I had sense enough to be scared.

Suddenly he dropped me. I crashed to the floor, hitting my head and my left knee. I screamed at the pain, unable to tell which place hurt worse.

To my utter amazement, a flash went off in my face. He was actually taking my picture! I struggled to get up.

"Keep quiet!" he growled. "I'm warning you. And don't try to get away."

He pulled the closet door open. I caught a quick glimpse of a room lined with shelves and full of yet more packing boxes.

That was all I saw before he grabbed me again.

"I'll be back," he hissed. "Don't go away."

He literally threw me into the closet. I thought it was a shame I wasn't Shannon—he'd never be able to toss her around like this.

Then I collided with the corner of a box and heard a crack. Pain shot along my right arm as I slithered to the floor. I couldn't get my breath, it hurt so badly.

In that instant Tree whipped the door shut, and I was in complete darkness.

I lay in a pathetic heap for a few minutes, shocked and scared. When I finally did try to get up, I found my knees so wobbly I could hardly stand. With each movement my arm screamed in agony.

I leaned against a box and tried to calm myself.

"I'll be back," he had said. The question was, when? And what was he going to do when he got here? I didn't want to find out.

"Help!" I yelled. "Help! Mr. Maples! Mr. Jones! Help!"

They wouldn't hear me, I knew, but I had to try. It was easier than beating the door down.

I tried to stare through the inky blackness, but I couldn't. I'd never seen darkness so thick. It made my stomach churn. So did the thought of spiders running around in here . . . spiders that I couldn't see.

If I could find the door, I would find the light switch. But in the instant darkness, my sense of direction was all out of whack. I had no idea where the door was.

I shuddered and pain ripped up my arm. Something was broken. It had to be. I'd heard a crack when I hit the box, and the bursts of pain every time my arm moved were terrible.

I ran my left hand carefully up my right arm. I couldn't feel any bones sticking out or anything, but the pain was very bad halfway between my elbow and shoulder. I rested my bad arm across my body and told myself not to move it while I searched for the door.

I took three steps and banged into the edge of a packing box. Automatically I reached out with my arms so I wouldn't fall, and I screamed. I couldn't help it; it hurt so badly.

I needed a sling to hold my arm still.

I needed a piece of material to make a sling. I needed to see to fold the material for the sling.

I needed two good hands to tie the sling.

I needed everything I didn't have.

Think, you wimp! Think!

God, You live here in East Edge! Help!

My T-shirt! It was the only material I had, so I decided to use it for a sling.

Very, very carefully I slipped my left arm out of its sleeve and dropped it down inside my shirt.

Very, very carefully I took hold of the bottom hem with my left hand and lifted the shirt up and over my head. The whole time, I kept my right arm pressed to my chest.

Very, very carefully I slid the shirt along my right arm and off. It only hurt when I pulled my arm away from my body to pass the material.

I was scared to death that Tree would pick this minute to throw the door open. I felt so helpless!

Quickly I put my shirt back over my head and thrust my left arm into its sleeve. I let the shirt fall on the outside of my right arm, still pressed against my body.

Then I grabbed the hem of the shirt and pulled all the material over to my left hip. I twisted the material around and around until it was so tight it began to coil in on itself. I twisted some more until finally the material was in a tight knot. I tucked the knot inside the shirt and let go. It stayed. Then I pushed the shirt up my middle until my arm could rest in the cradle of support it made.

Feeling pleased with my cleverness, I went back to my search for the door. I walked very carefully, sweeping my left arm back and forth in front of me. In a matter of seconds I was slapping a shelf. The closet, after all, wasn't that big. I followed the shelves until they broke for the door.

I slid my hands up and down the walls by the door, looking for a light switch. Nothing. How could there be a closet this big without a light?

I grabbed the doorknob and twisted. I pushed and pulled. I rattled. I kicked. I screamed. I even cried. But nothing happened. I remained locked in my black and scary prison.

Finally, exhausted, I leaned against the door and slid slowly to the floor. I landed with a thud that jarred my teeth and left me seeing stars.

Suddenly I realized that the darkness wasn't quite as black anymore. Thin cracks of light shone high on one wall. I blinked my eyes a couple of times, but the cracks of light remained.

I was looking at the outline of a boarded-up window.

I pulled myself to my feet and hurried to the light, scarcely noticing the various boxes I bounced off of on the way.

I stood on tiptoe and reached as high as I could,

but I came nowhere near the bottom of the window.
I pushed a packing box under the window and
climbed on it. Now I could reach the lower sill. I
climbed down and pushed another box to the
window.

When I realized that with one arm I couldn't
get the second box on top of the first, I felt like I
had run into a brick wall.

I had to find a way, and fast. Tree could return
at any minute.

I reached down, squatting like the weight lifters
I saw on TV, and tried to lift the second box from
the bottom, but it was too bulky and too heavy.
Maybe if I got rid of the heavy, I could manage the
bulky.

I put my fingers under the top flap of the box
and pulled. There was a small movement, but no
more. I slid my hand along the top of the box and
found it taped tightly shut. I traced a strip of tape
to its end and began picking at it.

I think it took forever, but finally I had enough
tape pulled lose to open the box. Inside were the
inevitable magazines. I pulled them out as quickly
as I could, tossing them over my shoulder, not
caring how or where they landed.

When the box was empty, I leaned down again

and put my good hand under it. I lifted but I wasn't at the center of the box, and it fell over. I pushed it into place again and, after carefully seeking the midpoint, lifted another time. I leaned my shoulder into the box to help control it.

Up, up, slowly, slowly. Suddenly the second box slid onto the first box. The combined structure was almost as tall as I was.

I reached up and grabbed the top edge of the upper box and tipped it toward me. I had to turn the box over so I'd have the bottom to stand on.

I made the boxes like steps, the top one resting against the wall, the bottom one sticking out a bit so I could climb onto it first. I was anything but graceful, and it hurt like crazy, but I made it to the top.

Now my head was even with the window. I looked very carefully at what was blocking the light, but it was hard to make out any details. I put out my hand and stuck it right into a cobweb.

I screamed and pulled back, almost overbalancing and going off backwards. My skin was clammy, and I felt things crawling on me where there were none. I just hate spiders . .. but I wasn't going to let them beat me!

I reached out again and slid my fingers along

the thin line of light, looking for a place to get a handhold. There was no gap. I pushed on the corners to see if I could make whatever was stuck in the window shimmy. It remained firm. The only bright spot was that I had swept away all the cobwebs.

Ignoring the tickling feeling on my arm, I slid my hand slowly back and forth across what felt like a board, searching for I didn't know what. What I found were two nails sticking out of the wood, one on either side, about four inches from the edge and halfway between top and bottom. Someone must have put them there like little handles.

If I had had two good hands, I could have taken hold and pulled, but I had only one. So I pulled a bit on the left nail and then I pulled a bit on the right nail. Little by little, ever so slowly, the board began to work loose.

I was sweating profusely by this time, both from fear and exertion. I could feel drops running down my back and my neck. My fingers were so sweaty that I had to keep wiping them on my shorts.

Suddenly I realized one of the drops of sweat wasn't running *down* my neck but *up,* up to my chin and toward my mouth. It *was* a spider, and he was aiming for my mouth!

I swatted wildly at my throat. I probably hurt myself more than I hurt the spider, but somehow in my frenzy, I knocked him away. It took me a while to get my breath back. I decided that someday, when I told this story to my grandchildren, I'd leave this part out.

I went back to the nails. The crack of light was getting bigger and bigger, and it was only a matter of time.

When the board suddenly came loose, I almost tumbled off the boxes. Somehow I kept my balance and stood there hugging the board, looking out at the beautiful, wonderful, gorgeous sunlight filtering through the very dirty window and at a large rhododendron bush just outside.

Now that I had light, it didn't take me long to find the lock on the bottom of the window and unfasten it. It was a wide, short window, and I thought I should be able to squirm out without too much trouble—once I was higher, that is.

I climbed down off my tower and grabbed a third box. Dumping the magazines and playing weight lifter again, I slid the third box onto box #1, beside box #2. I climbed onto #1 and slowly lifted #3 into place on #2. I turned #3 over, balanced it on #2, and climbed up.

I stuck my head out the window. I could see Brooke's house through the rhododendron branches. At that moment I was weary enough and scared enough that I would have been happy to see Brooke herself.

I reached out with my left hand and put my right knee on the window sill, ducked my head and folded myself in half, guarding my arm. By now it was feeling hot, and I knew it was swollen. Any time I bumped it or jostled it, knives sliced at my arm.

I was halfway out the window when hands closed around my ankle.

"Where do you think you're going?" Tree shouted.

My heart stopped beating, and I knew I was going to die on the spot.

Tree yanked on my ankle, trying to pull me back inside.

"No!" I screamed. "No!" I grabbed a rhododendron branch and held on as tightly as I could.

I kicked my leg, trying to get my foot free, but I was in such an awkward position that I couldn't put much force behind my kicks.

"Let go! Help!"

His hand closed around my other ankle. My knee was still balanced on the window sill, and he was tugging hard. I fought him for a few seconds, then suddenly stopped resisting.

He was pulling so hard that when I let him have my leg, he lost his balance and went over backwards. I felt him release me, then I heard the boxes falling. He landed on the closet floor with a very loud oomph!

I scrambled the rest of the way out of the window and found myself pinned to the side of the house by a small forest of rhododendrons. I dropped to my hands and knees and crawled under the bushes.

In the struggle with Tree, my sling had come undone, and my arm was throbbing worse than ever. I held it to my chest and ran for Brooke's house.

"Help!" I yelled as I ran. "Help! Brooke! Anybody! Help!"

"Stop!"

I looked around in surprise, and there was Tree whipping around the corner of Mr. Maples's house.

"You can't get away!" he screamed, gaining on me with each stride. He had such long legs!

I finally reached Brooke's front door and began ringing the doorbell and pounding.

"Help!" I yelled. "Help! Brooke! Mrs. Picardy! Natalie! Anybody!"

But no one came to my rescue.

Tree stopped just a few feet from me and smiled nastily. "They're not home, kid. I saw them leave."

He jumped toward me, and I jumped away. I was not going to let him catch me again!

I ran off the side of the porch into the area between the house and the shrubs. I figured I was small and could run in this narrow path faster than Tree.

He came crashing through the bushes after me. I thought of Mrs. Picardy's beautiful flowers and hoped she wouldn't be too upset by what Tree was doing to them.

I expected Tree's hand to grab me any minute. With every step I took, my arm bounced and stabbed with pain.

I came to the corner of the house. A great holly tree grew hard against the house, leaving no way for me to get past. I ran straight at it until the last second, then veered around it, hardly feeling the prickly leaves scratching against my arms and cheek. I shot through the opening in the hedge into the backyard.

Behind me I could hear Tree swearing as he ran into the holly tree going full speed. I grinned. It couldn't have happened to a more deserving person.

I ran to the far end of the pool and turned to face Tree. He had to come down one side or the other to get to me, and I could run him in circles around the pool all day if I needed to.

He charged through the hedge and came to a halt, staring across the pool at me.

"Don't think you're going to get away," he panted. He was still pulling holly leaves out of his T-shirt, and there were some scratches on his arms.

"What are you going to do to me, Tree? Kill me? That's the only thing that will keep me from telling people you're the one who burned the Restons' house and stole the dolls and the bike and chopped the table up. You even have pictures of everything."

"Pictures won't prove a thing," he said. "Anyone can have pictures."

"Of all the Restons' troubles? Of me lying on the floor? I don't know why you did all the things you did, but I know you did them."

"You think I won't kill you?" he said.

"I think you won't kill me," I said, not at all sure he wouldn't. "I think you didn't want to kill the Restons either. You just wanted to make their lives miserable for some reason."

"They made mine miserable!" he shouted. "All I

did was have some fun, and they hung me for it!"

"What are you talking about?"

"Mr. Reston was my principal. To celebrate finishing my senior finals, I broke a few windows at the high school. And he wouldn't let me come to graduation!"

"What did you expect him to do?" I said. "Congratulate you?"

He stared, furious at me and at life. "Then Mrs. Lady Cop Reston stopped me after a graduation party. She said I was driving drunk."

"Were you?"

Tree glared at me. "What's it to you?"

"So you were! What happened? Was it the first time? Did you lose your license?"

"For a whole year! And yes, it was the first time!"

"A year's not so long. It could have been worse, I guess."

"It is worse! My father took away my car and says he won't give it back. And he won't let me drive his until I'm twenty-one. I have to buy my own if I ever want to drive again. And my own insurance, too!"

"Sounds reasonable to me. At least you aren't in jail."

"I'm supposed to be, but there's not enough room. Instead I've got to go to classes for Accelerated Rehabilitation Development with a bunch of drunks!"

"Maybe it'll keep you from becoming one."

"None of this would have happened if the Restons had stayed out of my life!"

"So all this trouble is their fault?"

"Of course it is!" Tree shouted.

Suddenly I noticed that as he had been talking, he had been edging slowly along the side of the pool. If I weren't careful, he'd knock me in, and then I'd be in big trouble because of my arm.

"And finding those dolls and the bike is my fault, right?"

"You got it, kid!"

He made a lunge for me, but I was expecting his move and took off. I rounded the side of the house, heading for the street and people. But I cut the corner too closely, and my hair got tangled in the lilac bush as I tried to brush past. I was jerked to an abrupt halt.

With my good hand I grabbed at my hair and pulled and pulled. I didn't care how much it hurt or how much hair I lost. I had to get away!

Tree's evil laugh gave me goose bumps all over.

I looked over my shoulder, and there he was. I pulled harder.

"Let me help you, kid," he said and reached for me.

I screamed and screamed. "Don't you touch me! Help! Somebody, help!"

Suddenly Brooke and Mrs. Picardy came flying around the corner of the house.

"Help me!" I yelled.

I gave one final tug, and my hair came free. I ran to Mrs. Picardy and practically fell into her arms.

"Where were you ten minutes ago?" I asked. I was shaking all over, just like Cammi's mother.

"We just got home," Brooke said. "What's going on?"

"Eddie," Mrs. Picardy said, "what's going on?"

Eddie? Who was Eddie?

"I thought his name was Tree," I said.

"He's Edward T. Maples III," said Brooke. "The kids call him Tree because of Maples. Get it?"

I nodded, feeling very sad. "He's Mr. Maples's Eddie?"

Brooke nodded. "You're not afraid of Eddie, are you?" It was obvious what she thought of being afraid of Eddie.

I nodded, too tired to tell her about the closet, my arm, and the wild chase.

"He's the one who burned down the Restons' house," I said.

"Eddie?" said Mrs. Picardy. I noticed that she didn't look particularly surprised. Apparently she knew him better than Brooke. "Is that true?"

"No, no, of course not," he said. "You know me better than that!"

"I'm afraid it is true," said a sad and lonely voice.

I hadn't even noticed Mr. Maples until he spoke. He must have finally turned his hearing aid back on and heard me screaming. He certainly had heard what I said about Eddie. All the sparkle was gone from him, like a balloon deflated, leaving just a poor, tired old man.

"Eddie," he said, "when I heard the screaming, I called the police, only to find out that they were on their way over here to talk to me about you. They already knew you were guilty of setting the fire, and they're here for you."

The two policemen I had seen earlier at the Restons' house stepped out from behind the rhododendron.

Eddie took one look, panicked, turned, and ran.

He tripped over one of the lawn chairs by the pool and fell into the deep end. The policemen were waiting for him when he stumbled up the ladder. They took him away in handcuffs.

I sat in our backyard on a lounge, enjoying the sunshine and the attention. Cammi, Shannon, Bethany, and Alysha were visiting me, drinking tall glasses of Mom's great iced tea. If I so much as moved, they all jumped.

"What do you want?" they asked. "What can we get you? Do you need some more to drink? Some pretzels?"

It was almost worth the broken arm—but this was only my first day home from the hospital. I wondered how long I could manage to keep them so concerned.

"I'm so glad you weren't hurt any worse!" said Cammi. "I'd have felt so guilty, since our house was the reason."

She smiled at me, and I smiled back.

They had kept me in the hospital for two days until the swelling in my arm went down enough to be put in a cast, and Cammi had come to visit me there. We had talked a lot, and I had finally told her what Brooke had said.

"She said that?" Cammi had looked horrified. "Don't you believe a word of it! Not one word!"

I had sort of known deep down that Brooke was probably lying for some reason of her own, but it was so nice to hear Cammi confirm it.

Now she said, "I can't believe you were doing that job to earn money for us."

"I wanted to help. It's hard to figure out how to help when you're our age."

"Well, don't worry about a thing," Shannon said. "I called up Mr. Maples and asked if Bethany and Alysha and I could come finish the job. We'll put the money in the Restons' fund just like you were going to."

I was overwhelmed, and for once I couldn't think of anything to say.

"How is Mr. Maples?" I finally managed. "I feel so bad for him."

"He sounded sad, but he told me he remembered me and that I should plan to be a model some day because I was going to be beautiful." Shannon laughed at the thought, but it sounded just like something Mr. Maples would say.

"I feel sort of left out," said Cammi. "Can I help even if the money's for us?"

We all looked at her and didn't know what to say. If she helped, then it wasn't the same somehow.

"Please?" She looked so forlorn.

"Hey," I said, "you aren't crying anymore!"

"Nope. I decided that so many nice things had happened to our family since the fire that life's not so bad after all. If Bugs would just show up, everything would be great."

I looked at the girls sitting around me. They were new friends, and I liked them, and apparently they liked me in spite of what Brooke said. But I didn't know them well yet. I didn't know how they'd take my latest idea.

"I have an idea," I said. "And it'll help you feel better, Cammi. Let's have a club—the Kids Care Club. We can do all kinds of things for people and put some or all of the money in the church's Help Fund. If there's a big need, we can put all the money in, but if there's not, we can keep part to use for ourselves."

Everyone looked at me without saying a word. I

felt nervous. They obviously thought it was a terrible idea, and I knew they would send me back to Indiana if they could.

And just like that, I realized I wanted to stay in Pennsylvania. Not that I disliked Indiana. I just understood suddenly what Dad meant about change. Sometimes it seems bad, but it doesn't have to be. And God, who never changes, lived here in East Edge, too, to help me with the changes.

Suddenly the girls all exploded.

"What a great idea!" yelled Alysha, bouncing up and down in her chair. "I love it!"

"Dee, yes! Yes, yes, yes!" said Bethany.

"I think it's the best thing I've heard in a long time," said Shannon. "I nominate Dee for president of the Kids Care Club!"

Cammi rushed over and gave me a hug. "I second it," she said. "I'm so glad you moved here."

EAST EDGE #2 MYSTERIES

Be sure to read about Cammi's adventures in East Edge Mystery #2 *Discovery at Denny's Deli*

"Where have you been?" Mrs. Wells hissed, her voice all angry. She didn't sound at all like the pleasant person I'd talked with at tea just a few minutes before. "Are you crazy, going out like that? What if somebody sees you?"

"Shut up!" the man said.

I'd never heard such a nasty tone of voice, not even on TV.

"I don't need you telling me what to do and what not to do! If I want to go out, I'll go out. So just butt out and shut up! Nobody saw me!"

The door slammed, the noise echoing in the empty lobby.

Who was Mrs. Wells really? Where did she come from? Was she a nice person or a nasty one?

One thing I was sure of. Mrs. Wells had lied when she told me she lived alone.